NUTRITION AND HEALTH

LIFE AS A VEGETARIAN

EATING WITHOUT MEAT

BY JASON BRAINARD

Portions of this book originally appeared in
Vegetarianism by Susan M. Traugh.

LUCENT
PRESS

Published in 2020 by
Lucent Press, an Imprint of Greenhaven Publishing, LLC
353 3rd Avenue
Suite 255
New York, NY 10010

Designer: Deanna Paternostro
Editor: Jennifer Lombardo

Cataloging-in-Publication Data

Names: Brainard, Jason.
Title: Life as a vegetarian: eating without meat / Jason Brainard.
Description: New York : Lucent Press, 2020. | Series: Nutrition and health | Includes index.
Identifiers: ISBN 9781534568853 (pbk.) | ISBN 9781534568723 (library bound) | ISBN 9781534568808 (ebook)
Subjects: LCSH: Vegetarianism–Juvenile literature.
Classification: LCC TX392.B728 2020 | DDC 641.5'636–dc23

Printed in China

Some of the images in this book illustrate individuals who are models. The depictions do not imply actual situations or events.

CPSIA compliance information: Batch #BW20KL: For further information contact Greenhaven Publishing LLC, New York, New York at 1-844-317-7404.

Please visit our website, www.greenhavenpublishing.com. For a free color catalog of all our high-quality books, call toll free 1-844-317-7404 or fax 1-844-317-7405.

CONTENTS

FOREWORD

People often want to do whatever they can to live healthy lives, but this is frequently easier said than done. For example, experts suggest minimizing stress as it takes a long-term toll on the body and mind. However, in an era where young adults must balance school attendance, extracurricular and social activities, and several hours of homework each night, stress is virtually unavoidable. Socioeconomic factors also come into play, which can prevent someone from making good health choices even when they are aware of what the consequences will be.

Other times, however, the problem is misinformation. The media frequently reports watered-down versions of scientific findings, distorting the message and causing confusion. Sometimes multiple conflicting results are reported, leaving people to wonder whether a simple action such as eating dark chocolate is helpful, harmful, or has no effect on their health at all. In such an environment, many people ignore all health news and decide for themselves what the best course of action is. This has led to dangerous trends such as the recent anti-vaccination movement.

The titles in the Nutrition and Health series aim to give young adults the information they need to take charge of their health. Factual, unbiased text presents all sides of current health issues with the understanding that everyone is different and knows their own body and health needs best. Readers also gain insight into important nutrition topics, such as whether a vegetarian diet is right for them, which foods may improve or exacerbate any existing health issues, and precautions they can take to prevent the spread of foodborne illnesses.

Annotated quotes from medical experts provide accurate and accessible explanations of challenging concepts, as well as different points of view on controversial issues. Additional books and websites are listed, giving readers a starting point from which to delve deeper into specific topics that are of interest to them. Full-color photographs, fact boxes, and enlightening charts are presented alongside the informative text to give young adults a clearer picture of today's most pressing health concerns.

With so much complicated and conflicting information about nutrition and health available on social media and in the news, it can be hard for all people—but especially for young adults—to make smart choices about their health. However, this series presents an accessible approach to health education that makes the work of staying healthy seem much less intimidating.

HOLD THE MEAT!

As the science of nutrition evolves, more and more people are experimenting with their diets in an attempt to be healthier. While many people have chosen to eat more vegetables, fruit, and whole grains, others have taken another step and stopped eating meat. A 2018 Gallup poll found that 5 percent of those living in the United States considered themselves to be vegetarians. The same poll found that 3 percent of respondents had given up eating any animal products and identified as being vegan. These numbers have changed very little over the last 20 years.

There are several reasons why a person may choose not to eat meat. All of them are personal. Many do so as part of an attempt to have a healthier diet. Others stop eating meat to protest the animal cruelty that is common in modern industrial farming. Still others forgo eating meat to help the environment. Some people do it for all three reasons. While it may seem like everyone is suddenly going vegetarian or vegan, these diet choices have been around for centuries.

A Brief History of Vegetarianism

Throughout history, certain groups of people have avoided eating meat for philosophical or religious reasons. People in ancient India and Greece followed a vegetarian diet as part of their belief in nonviolence toward all living things. Indians, Buddhists, and Hindus practiced vegetarianism because of a belief in the sacredness of all living creatures. The Hindu belief in reincarnation—the return of a human soul into a new body, which was sometimes an animal's—contributed to the desire to avoid eating the flesh of any creature.

During the time of the Roman Empire—around 27 BC to AD 476—vegetarianism was not widespread in Europe. However, it began to gain favor centuries later as certain religious groups embraced it during the Renaissance, which began in the 14th century and lasted until the 17th century. In colonial America, small groups of people practiced vegetarianism, including Benjamin Franklin. Although later in life Franklin returned to eating meat, other Americans persisted with their vegetarian practice. Most American vegetarians in the 18th and 19th centuries belonged to various religious groups that advocated a meat-free diet because they considered the way in which animals were slaughtered to be

Benjamin Franklin, who was a vegetarian when it was not common in most societies, wrote that he followed this diet because he felt better when he ate less meat and saved both money and time from not buying it.

inhumane. These groups included the Ephrata Cloister, the Bible Christian Church, the Grahamites, and the Seventh-Day Adventist Church. Today, most Seventh-Day Adventists continue to follow a vegetarian diet. At the time, the health and environmental issues associated with eating meat were largely unknown, and modern "factory farming" had not become widespread, so religion was by far the main reason why people became vegetarians.

Vegetarianism gained more widespread recognition in Europe and the United States in 1847 with the formation of the Vegetarian Society of the United Kingdom in England. This organization was formed by a group of Christians who were opposed to eating meat because they believed it was cruel to animals. The society, which advocated a "live and let live" philosophy toward all creatures and even promoted alternatives to leather shoes, soon spread to other parts of Europe. In 1908, the vegetarian diet gained worldwide popularity when the International Vegetarian Union was founded in Germany. Like the Vegetarian Society, the International Vegetarian Union advocated abstaining from eating meat for moral reasons. This organization still operates today, bringing together people from all over the world to promote vegetarianism.

Just as people have done throughout history, people today are choosing vegetarianism for a variety of reasons, including religious, moral, nutritional, and philosophical concerns. However, before giving up on a major source of protein and certain vitamins and minerals, budding vegetarians need to do their research and educate themselves on basic nutrition to help them stay healthy.

Chapter One

FAR FROM A FAD

Getting a group of friends or family members to agree on where and what to eat for a meal is often challenging. Taking into account different tastes, individual food allergies or intolerances, various self-imposed dietary restrictions, and economic concerns, it can be a long time before everyone in the group is satisfied with the food options. Luckily for vegetarians, most restaurants these days have meat-free choices on the menu and many home-cooked meals can be easily adapted to suit their needs. Today, increasing numbers of people are embracing a plant-based diet. In addition to true vegetarians, a much larger group is reducing meat consumption and eating meatless meals on a more regular basis. A growing number of people do not identify themselves as vegetarian but nevertheless occasionally eat vegetarian meals. Eating a plant-based diet is a trend that has grown in popularity in recent years, both in the United States and around the world.

Subsets of Vegetarianism

Vegetarians are not one defined group of people, but rather come from all walks of life. Similarly, no single vegetarian diet exists. Instead, vegetarianism includes many different eating philosophies, and there can be variations in how strictly someone follows their vegetarian diet. A vegetarian diet can mean any of the following options:

- lacto-ovo vegetarian: Lacto means "milk." Ovo means "egg." This group eats a plant-based diet as well as dairy products and eggs, but does not eat meat, including birds and fish.
- lacto vegetarian: This group eats a plant-based diet and adds dairy products to that diet. They do not eat eggs, meat, fish, or poultry.

A vegetarian meal can be delicious, filling, and enjoyable.

- ovo vegetarian: This group supplements a plant-based diet with eggs but does not eat dairy, meat, fish, or poultry.
- pesco-vegetarians, or pescatarians: This group eats a plant-based diet and no meat except fish. Generally, they also eat dairy and eggs.
- semi-vegetarian, or partial vegetarian: This group tends to exclude red meat but eats most other foods, including eggs, dairy, fish, and poultry.

Today, popular culture is altering the classic definition of vegetarianism with less common, more specific dietary labels. Flexitarians are people who mostly eat vegetarian. Pollo-vegetarians, or pollotarians, do not eat meat or fish but do eat poultry. Although not technically vegetarians, these people nevertheless may define themselves as vegetarians.

A Closer Look

Broadly speaking, meat is any kind of animal flesh. However, the word "meat" is generally used to describe red meat, which comes mainly from cows, pigs, and sheep, although horse, goat, and bison mcat also falls into this category. White meat includes fish and poultry, which describes meat from birds, including chicken, duck, turkey, and goose.

Not everyone is very strict with their vegetarian diet. Christy Pugh, a bookkeeper from New Hampshire, is one example. Although she normally follows a vegetarian diet, her meals sometimes include one of her favorite foods: organic turkey sausage.

In addition to vegetarians, many people are vegan. Many people transition slowly to veganism by becoming vegetarian first. However, veganism is generally viewed less as a dietary choice and more as a complete lifestyle. They eat only plant based foods and shun all animal products, including meat, fish, poultry, dairy, and eggs; many also exclude honey because bees make it. In addition, many vegans do not use any animal products, such as leather, fur, wool, or silk. Vegans try to use cruelty-free products whenever possible, meaning that their personal care items are not tested on animals and do not contain animal products. For instance, a vegan would not use a down comforter because down is the term for a soft layer of feathers on geese. They also tend to avoid items that contain latex, such as latex gloves, because a milk protein called casein is sometimes used to process latex. Because of their concern for the environment, they also try to use plant-based household cleaning items, including dish soap and laundry detergent.

A vegan lifestyle extends to caring about the suffering of other humans as well. For this reason, many vegans avoid products such as coffee, chocolate, and tea that do not contain a Fair Trade label, which indicates that the product was not made through unethical practices, including child labor. Those who might be able to afford gold and diamonds also tend to avoid

Shown here is a child laborer working on a coffee plantation. To avoid exploiting children, vegans try to buy coffee and other food items that carry the Fair Trade label, which certifies that the company uses fair and ethical methods.

them because of human rights violations in their production. The 2006 movie *Blood Diamond* brought to the public's attention many of the problems with diamond mines in particular. The list of products that vegans must choose carefully can seem endless; vegan paint, vegan juice, vegan food coloring, and much more are all available, but they can be difficult to find and more expensive than the same items that are made traditionally. This makes a fully vegan lifestyle less accessible for people who are on a tight budget.

Vegetarian and Vegan Statistics

According to a 2016 survey from the Vegetarian Resource Group conducted by Harris Interactive, 37 percent of American adults always or sometimes eat vegetarian meals when dining out. Based on this study, more than 90 million adults in the United States enjoy having a vegetarian meal when dining out but may not consider themselves vegetarians. Steven, a teacher and father of three, said, "I do eat meat, although not as often as I used to. When I'm out, I like to get something that feels healthy and special. Whether it's spicy eggplant or a really exotic salad, I enjoy ordering dishes that I couldn't or wouldn't make at home."[1]

This same Harris Interactive survey found that 43 percent of the youngest adults polled enjoyed having a vegetarian meal when dining out, suggesting that younger people were more likely than their elders to choose vegetarian meals. According to the KidsHealth website, "Preteens and teens often voice their independence through the foods they choose to eat. One strong statement is the decision to stop eating meat. This is common among teens, who may decide to embrace vegetarianism in support of animal rights, for health reasons, or because friends are doing it."[2]

Some people are more likely to become vegetarian or vegan than others. Harris Interactive fielded a survey for the Vegetarian Resource Group to determine what types of people become vegetarian. They interviewed U.S. adults nationwide and weighted the results based on region, gender, age, education, household income, ethnicity, and time spent online.

The survey found that people who consider themselves vegetarians come from all categories of American life. Students are the largest group, with 15 percent of high school and college students defining themselves as vegetarian. More females than males follow a vegetarian diet. The East and West Coasts also contain a larger percentage of vegetarians than the middle of the country.

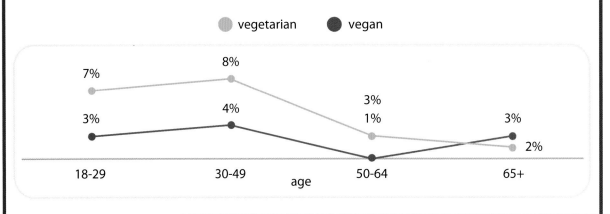

Ages of American Vegans and Vegetarians

● vegetarian ● vegan

	18-29	30-49	50-64	65+

vegetarian: 7%, 8%, 3%, 2%
vegan: 3%, 4%, 1%, 3%

age

Older people are less likely to be either vegetarian or vegan, as this information from Gallup shows.

A 2018 Gallup poll of Americans measured the political leanings of those who considered themselves to be vegetarian or vegan. Only 2 percent of respondents identifying as conservative claimed to be vegetarian or vegan. In contrast, 16 percent of liberals stated they were vegetarian or vegan. This may be partially because liberals are more likely to report animal welfare and environmentalism among their top concerns.

A Closer Look

According to *Vegetarian Times*, fruitarians are people who eat only the parts of a plant that can be easily replaced, such as fruit, nuts, and tomatoes.

A Personal Choice

It is clear from the number of different kinds of vegetarianism that not all vegetarians want to completely give up meat. Some people may just want to eat less meat or stop eating certain kinds of meat. Are they vegetarians, then? *Vegetarian Times* magazine is clear about its opinion. In 2002, the organization stated, "For many people who are working to become vegetarians, chicken and fish may be transitional foods, but they are not vegetarian foods … the word 'vegetarian' means someone who eats no meat, fish or chicken."[3] However, many others see the label as more flexible—a guideline rather than a strict rule. Pugh explained, "Sometimes I feel like I'm a bad vegetarian, that I'm not strict enough or good enough. I really like vegetarian food but I'm just not 100 percent committed."[4] Some people who will only eat meat products very rarely or will only eat specific ones may say they are vegetarian to avoid confusion at communal meals; for example, if they are invited to dinner by a friend who wants to know their dietary preferences, they may find it easier to just say they are vegetarian than to list all the foods they try to avoid.

Not too long ago, a salad was one of the only things a vegetarian or vegan could find on a restaurant menu or premade in the supermarket. Today, there are many more offerings.

Whether they are true vegetarians or "flexitarians," people all across the United States are changing the way they eat—and these health-conscious changes are being reflected in the marketplace.

Freedom of Choice

Vegetarians are bringing their food preferences to their local restaurants and stores. In 2015, Suitable Brands (SB), a company that helps brands meet customers' expectations, reported on a survey that found 81 percent of consumers were willing to make sacrifices—such as giving up meat—to address social and environmental issues. In 2017, SB reported on another study that found that 86 percent of consumers expect brands to take an active role in addressing such issues. To appeal to this huge portion of con-sumers and attract more customers, many brands have started making and selling vegetarian and vegan food options.

A few years ago, any fast food restaurant would have been off-limits for a vegetarian because its meat-saturated menu would have provided few or no choices for people following a plant-based diet. However, that is chang-ing, in large part because beef consumption is down in the United States from its high in 1976. Back then, Americans ate about 94 pounds (42.6 kg) of beef each year. According to the United States Department of Agricul-ture (USDA), by 2017, per-person consumption of beef had fallen below 50 pounds (22.7 kg) a year. As more and more people move away from eating beef and other types of red meat, vegetarian offerings are becoming commonplace in many restaurants all over the country. Burger King, for example, now offers the Impossible Whopper. It meets the requirements of a strict vegetarian diet while providing the texture and taste of real beef.

The aisles of America's grocery stores are also changing. Vegetarian foods used to occupy a small "health foods" section, but now plant-based meat substitutes and vegetarian-friendly foods are displayed in nearly ev-ery aisle. In fact, a 2018 report from Supermarket News stated that plant-based food sales had increased an astounding 20 percent in the previous year, making the total amount of money spent on plant-based foods in the previous 12 months $3.3 billion.

Many consumers are pleased by the changes they see in grocery stores. Reed Mangels, a registered dietician and the mother of three teenage vegetarians, is one such individual. She said, "We visit my parents in north-ern Florida once a year. When we first started going 15 years ago, we'd

Militant Veganism

While most vegans respect other lifestyle choices, a small part of the community uses guilt and shame to make non-vegans feel bad about their lifestyle. Instead of turning people toward veganism, however, such tactics frequently have the opposite effect. In an article on the website Lakota People's Law Project, vegan Rylee McCallin wrote, "I believe a lack of understanding and respect from these 'militant vegans' can give the rest of the community a bad reputation."[1] McCallin noted that some cultures, including most Native American groups, have religious and cultural ties to hunting and meat-eating, and she believes it is wrong to force these groups to give up their traditions.

Even if someone is not a member of a Native American nation, they may not be willing or able to completely give up animal products. When vegans accuse these people of being immoral, it can cause resentment. The organization People for the Ethical Treatment of Animals (PETA) is frequently the target of outrage for this reason. PETA's ads and protests use strong sentiments to get people's attention, but these often backfire and create more resentment. For example, in 2003 and 2004, PETA toured college campuses and other venues with an exhibit promoting a vegan lifestyle. The campaign, called "Holocaust on Your Plate," argued that eating meat and wearing leather were morally the same as the murder of millions of Jewish people and other victims during the Holocaust. To make its point, PETA compared photos of chickens kept in factory farm cages to starving inmates of German concentration camps. Other images and exhibit text compared slaughtered animals to murdered Jewish people.

These comparisons caused outrage, especially among the Jewish community. "The effort by PETA to compare the deliberate, systematic murder of millions of Jews to the issue of animal rights is abhorrent,"[2] the Anti-Defamation League stated. Ethicist Wesley J. Smith agreed: "That PETA can't distinguish between the unspeakable evil of the Shoah [the Holocaust] and animal husbandry reveals a perverted sense of moral values that is almost beyond comprehension."[3] Vegans tend to have more success promoting their lifestyle when they show respect and understanding for alternate lifestyles.

1. Rylee McCallin, "Native Tradition v. Militant Veganism," Lakota People's Law Project, December 12, 2018. www.lakotalaw.org/news/2018-12-12/veganism.

2. Quoted in David Teacher, "'Holocaust on a Plate' Angers US Jews," *Guardian*, March 3, 2003. www.theguardian.com/media/2003/mar/03/advertising.marketingandpr.

3. Wesley J. Smith, "PETA to Cannibals: Don't Let Them Eat Steak," SFGate, December 21, 2003. www.sfgate.com/opinion/article/PETA-to-cannibals-Don-t-let-them-eat-steak-2507963.php.

pack an entire suitcase with soy milk and other foods. Now I don't bring anything. The local grocery chain has a good selection of vegetarian foods, which is significant because it's not a particularly progressive community."[5]

Changes such as these are also good news for vegetarians when they visit a restaurant. "What's nice," explained a vegetarian named Elisabeth, "is that I can go to the store or a fast food place with my friends and easily pick up foods that make us all happy. I might have a veggie burger while my boyfriend has a chicken sandwich. It's nice to have that kind of selection."[6]

Veggie burgers and other meat substitutes have become so common that such foods are even included in diabetic diet plans. In the 2003 edition of the American Dietetic Association/American Diabetes Exchange diet, one line was devoted to meat substitutes for people trying to stick to a low-fat diet to control their diabetes. In contrast, the Academy of Nutrition and Dietetics now maintains several webpages full of information on plant-based proteins, including veggie bacon and burgers, edamame (soybeans), tempeh (fermented soybeans), hummus (a pureed chickpea spread), soy sausage, and soy-based chicken nuggets.

Whether it is in mainstream diet recommendations, restaurants across the country, or the local supermarket, vegetarian foods are becoming more and more common. This is good news for vegetarians, non-vegetarians, and everyone in between who wants to eat a meat-free meal.

A Growing Industry

The growth in the vegetarian food market has also led to a rise in the number of companies in the food industry that are producing vegan foods. Items such as cashew cheese, soy milk, and egg substitutes are not as hard to find as they were a few years ago. Among the growing number of companies that produce such foods are Beyond Meat, Morningstar Farms, Turtle Island Foods, Eden Foods, Amy's Foods, and many others. Traditional brand-name food companies have also created

Veggie burgers have come a long way. Some now even have the same texture and taste as ground meat.

vegetarian and vegan options, such as Kraft Foods' Boca Burger.

As the range of vegetarian options continues to grow, greater availability will attract more people to these foods, whether someone eats vegan and vegetarian products every day or only once in a while. However, attracting customers depends on several factors: Great tasting meals that are convenient and reasonably priced will help drive additional expansion of the vegetarian foods market.

A Closer Look

According to the National Institutes of Health (NIH), more than 300,000 Americans die from diseases related to obesity each year.

Although it is difficult to determine exactly how many people stick to a strict vegetarian diet, the trend is clear: People are increasingly turning to plant-based diets, and the demand for vegetarian and vegan food is being met by restaurants, stores, and food producers alike.

Chapter Two

WHY GIVE UP MEAT?

People choose vegetarianism for many different reasons—for example, to improve their health or because they believe it is wrong to eat animals. Many choose to stop eating meat for a combination of reasons.

The final push to change their diet may be different for everyone. One person might research vegetarianism based on a medical professional's advice; another might discover that there are environmental benefits to eating less meat; photographs of slaughterhouses might turn a third's stomach. Whatever the reason, choosing to be a vegetarian is a personal decision that someone must make for themselves.

A Healthy Weight

As obesity rates have risen in the United States, some people have turned to a vegetarian diet in the belief that it can help keep the pounds off, and some research supports this. A large number of scientific studies have focused on veganism. One study, conducted in 2019 at Loma Linda University, involved examining the eating habits of 840 people. Researchers found that vegans had a lower body mass index (BMI) than either vegetarians or meat-eaters. The vegan participants' blood also contained a greater amount of several cancer-fighting nutrients than that of non-vegans.

Other research has supported these findings. Susan E. Berkow and Neal Barnard of the Physicians Committee for Responsible Medicine, a nonprofit group of doctors that completes independent research, reviewed 87 previous studies on veganism and vegetarianism. Their analysis showed that a low-fat vegan diet led to a weight loss of about 1 pound (0.45 kg) per week—a healthy rate of weight loss—without additional exercise or limits on portions. However, exercise is recommended for everyone no matter what their diet is like, as it has many benefits beyond weight loss.

Berkow and Barnard also analyzed studies that focused on vegetarianism and found that only about 6 percent of vegetarians were overweight. In several of the studies they reviewed, researchers had attempted to control for other healthy lifestyle factors. Were vegetarians thinner because they practiced a healthier lifestyle overall, or was their diet the main factor in weight control? By controlling for exercise, alcohol consumption,

Vegetables and fruit can help people lose weight while still feeling full.

and other factors, researchers believe they were able to point to diet as a significant factor in weight control.

Not only can vegetarians lose unhealthy weight, they also often keep it off. In a five-year study, physician Dean Ornish found that overweight people following a low-fat vegetarian diet lost an average of 24 pounds (11 kg) the first year and still kept the weight off 5 years later. They did not count calories or measure portions; they simply stayed on a vegetarian whole foods diet, meaning they did not eat processed foods.

Bad Cholesterol and Heart Disease

Weight loss alone is not the only reason why some people turn to a vegetarian diet to improve their health. According to the Centers for Disease Control and Prevention (CDC), heart disease kills an estimated 610,000 Americans each year, making it the number one cause of death in the United States. A significant number of studies show that a low-fat vegetarian diet can reduce the risk of heart disease by lowering a type of cholesterol called low-density lipoprotein (LDL). This is frequently referred to as "bad" cholesterol. A plant-based diet can also raise a person's levels of high-density lipoprotein (HDL), or "good," cholesterol.

Cholesterol is a waxy substance that is made in the liver and also obtained from animal products. Each cell membrane of the human body contains cholesterol and could not function properly without it. Cholesterol also helps digest fats.

When there is too much LDL cholesterol in the body, though, it starts to deposit itself on the walls of arteries. Its waxy texture allows it to stick together and form a substance called plaque. As plaque builds up, it narrows the passageway for blood flow. Eventually, it can completely block an artery. When the blockage prevents blood flow to the heart, it causes a heart attack; when it prevents blood flow to the brain, it causes a stroke. Both heart attack and stroke involve parts of the affected organ's tissue dying. If someone survives, they can suffer long-term health problems afterward.

Changes in diet can affect the amount of cholesterol in the body. According to the website Healthline, recent studies have found that cholesterol that comes from food does not generally make a difference to a person's health because for most people, when they eat high-cholesterol foods, their liver compensates by producing less of its own cholesterol. However, fat intake can affect a person's cholesterol levels, either positively or negatively. Saturated fats from animal products such as red meat and butter prompt the liver to produce more LDL cholesterol. In contrast, unsaturated fats, which come from plants such as avocados and nuts as well as from fish, prompt the production of HDL cholesterol. HDL cholesterol binds with LDL cholesterol and moves it out of the bloodstream, clearing artery blockages and naturally lowering a person's levels of LDL cholesterol. This can have a major positive effect on the health of the heart. According to a 2018 paper published by the American College of Cardiology, even a modest drop in LDL cholesterol can decrease a person's chance of developing heart disease.

The elimination of red meat and other foods high in saturated fat, such as dairy products, is generally one of the first things a doctor will suggest to patients with high cholesterol. They will often also suggest eating more plants that are high in fiber, such as broccoli, beans, seeds, and apples. Fiber is a material that humans cannot digest, which actually makes it helpful. There are two types of fiber: soluble and insoluble. Soluble fiber dissolves in water, so it is absorbed by the body and passes into the blood. This type of fiber can prevent constipation (difficulty having a bowel movement) because when it combines with feces, this fiber helps hold water in, keeping feces soft so it can pass through the intestines easily. Because soluble fiber binds with cholesterol and carries it out of the body, a lack of this type of

It is wise to speak with a licensed medical professional before starting a vegetarian diet.

fiber can contribute to high cholesterol levels and increase the risk of heart disease.

Insoluble fiber, as its name implies, does not dissolve in water. Because it cannot be digested, it is not absorbed by the body but instead moves through the intestines, pushing feces along and scraping the walls of the intestines clean. By pushing food through the intestines, insoluble fiber helps the body eliminate waste and toxins that would otherwise build up in the intestines as well as elsewhere in the body.

Red meat seems to be the biggest culprit in raising cholesterol levels, although butter and ice cream are also major contributors. According to a report by the Physicians Committee for Responsible Medicine, eating a plant-based diet may reduce a person's risk of developing heart disease by as much as 40 percent. A big reason for this appears to be the lower levels of LDL cholesterol found in the blood of those limiting meat consumption.

A Closer Look

According to the American Heart Association, one Burger King Whopper contains an entire day's worth of saturated fat.

Taking Care of a Young Heart

The benefits of avoiding saturated fat begin early in life. By cutting back on saturated fat, young people can keep their arteries clear and protect their cardiovascular health. The Coronary Artery Risk Development in Young Adults Study, a 20-year study, followed 5,000 18- to 30-year-olds and found that vegetarianism was linked to an increase in cardiovascular health and a decrease in the risk of heart disease.

Scientists now know that plaque buildup in arteries begins young. In fact, around the turn of the 21st century, doctors began to notice a startling new trend: an increase in the numbers of children and teens developing cardiovascular disease. Doctors previously assumed that heart disease was a health risk only for older and middle-aged Americans, not kids. According to a 2008 study, many obese children and teens have arteries that look similar to those of the average 45-year-old. Some estimates state that as many as 1 in 10 teens suffer from metabolic syndrome, which is defined as having at least three of the following risk factors: too much fat around the waist, high blood pressure, high blood sugar, high levels of fat in the blood, and abnormal cholesterol levels. People with metabolic syndrome are at very high risk for developing cardiovascular disease, stroke, or type 2 diabetes. In a study of 375 second and third graders, 5 percent already had metabolic syndrome and

Liam Hemsworth and Miley Cyrus are just two of many famous vegetarians.

45 percent had at least one risk factor for metabolic syndrome. University of Miami researcher Sarah Messiah warned,

> If a kid is age 8 with metabolic syndrome, it will take 10 years or less for that child to become a type 2 diabetic or develop heart disease … So as these kids enter adulthood, they could be faced with an entire life of chronic disease … It is sad because these children are so young and I don't know if they have ever really known what feeling good feels like.[7]

Several things young adults can do to avoid this condition include eating a healthy diet, exercising regularly, and avoiding tobacco and alcohol.

Ruth Frechman, a registered dietician, offered more information on what constitutes a healthy diet. She said that although the hazards of cholesterol-raising foods are well known, certain foods—including fatty fish, walnuts, oatmeal, and oat bran—can make a big impact on lowering cholesterol levels. These are all major components of a healthy vegetarian or pescatarian diet. Becoming a vegetarian is not the only way someone can eat healthily, but research has shown that a plant-based diet is one of the healthiest options.

Diabetes and Meat

Diabetes is diagnosed in two main categories: type 1 and type 2. Type 1 is an autoimmune disease, which means the immune system makes a mistake and starts attacking healthy body parts. In people with type 1 diabetes, the immune system attacks and destroys cells in the pancreas, an organ that produces insulin. Insulin is the body chemical that regulates blood sugar, or glucose, which comes from food.

Glucose is the only energy source for the brain. It is absorbed through the intestinal walls into the bloodstream, and then it travels to every part of the body. A healthy pancreas produces just the right amount of insulin around the clock, based on the amount of glucose circulating in the bloodstream. However, if the pancreas cannot make insulin or if the body cannot use the insulin it produces, the glucose cannot get into the cells. It stays in the bloodstream, keeping blood sugar levels high and causing damage to the organs in the body. For instance, a diabetes patient's eyes can be damaged by high blood sugar causing blockages in the tiny blood vessels and preventing enough oxygen from reaching the eyes. This can lead to blindness.

Diet and weight do not contribute to the development of type 1 diabetes. Experts are not sure exactly what causes the immune system to start attacking the pancreas, but they know that even people with the healthiest diets can develop it. However, a healthy diet, along with regular injections of insulin, is essential in helping someone with type 1 diabetes manage their condition.

Unlike type 1, type 2 diabetes is caused by excess weight, poor diet, and too little exercise. It is much more common than type 1; about

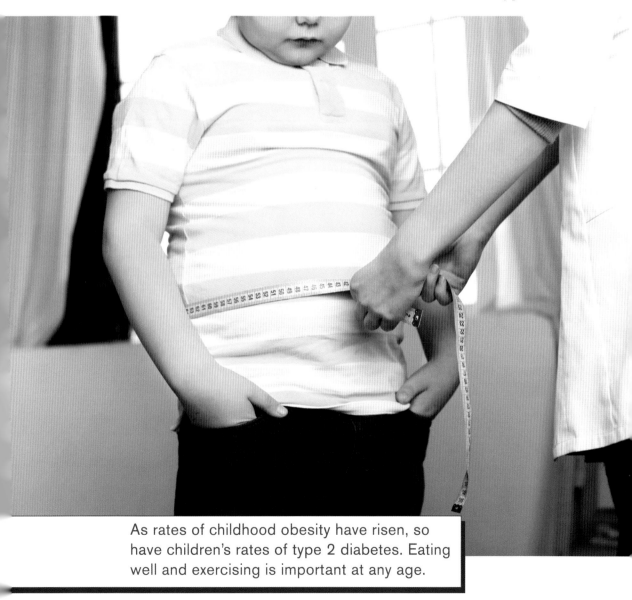

As rates of childhood obesity have risen, so have children's rates of type 2 diabetes. Eating well and exercising is important at any age.

95 percent of adults with diabetes have type 2. With this type of diabetes, the pancreas can make insulin, but the body cannot use it properly, so glucose cannot get into the cells. This condition is called insulin resistance. The blood glucose builds up to dangerous levels and starts to produce symptoms of diabetes. In the past, most people with type 2 diabetes were adults, so it used to be called adult-onset diabetes. However, as more children began developing this version of diabetes, that term has fallen out of use.

Type 2 diabetes can take many years to develop. People in this developing stage are called prediabetic—their blood glucose levels are higher than normal but not yet in the diabetic range. They are becoming insulin resistant and will develop diabetes unless they take steps to stop the process.

Many people have the mistaken idea that eating too much sugar causes diabetes. Since diabetes used to be called sugar disease and glucose is often called blood sugar, it is easy to see the reason for this mistake. However, evidence shows that simply eating a lot of sugar does not cause diabetes. According to family practitioner John Messmer, "A much bigger problem is that people are substituting refined sugar for fresh food and consuming sugary foods rather than whole grains, fruits and vegetables. Whole grain bread is better than donuts, whole grain cereal is better than sugary kids' cereals, and fresh fruit is better than syrup laden canned fruit."[8]

In fact, the saturated fat in red meat is a much bigger contributor to type 2 diabetes than sugar is. According to an article by Dr. Rosane Oliveira on the University of California (UC) Davis Integrative Medicine website, fat is the main contributor to insulin resistance. As fat builds up inside cells, it blocks the insulin-signaling process, causing blood sugar levels to increase. The pancreas starts releasing extra insulin to try to overcome this resistance, but the higher levels of insulin contribute to an accumulation of fat in the liver, which in turn makes that organ resistant to insulin. The liver tries to compensate by putting its fat back into the bloodstream, where it accumulates in the pancreas, killing the beta cells that are responsible for insulin production. Oliveira summed up, "Unable to defeat the insulin resistance or to produce higher amounts of insulin, our body's blood sugar levels go (and remain) up. And we have type 2 diabetes."[9]

Some studies have shown a link between meat consumption and an increased risk of developing type 2 diabetes. For example, a study called the Adventist Health Study-2 observed 89,000 people over 50 years. When it was published in 2013, it noted that "those who eat meat one or more days a week have significantly higher rates of diabetes"[10] than those who eat no meat at all. The more often people eat meat, the higher their risk rises. However, it is important to remember that eating meat is not a guarantee that someone will develop diabetes. A number of other factors come into play, such as the rest of the foods that make up a person's diet, how often they exercise, and whether other people in their family have diabetes. Someone who has several family members with diabetes is predisposed to developing it themselves, which means their risk is already higher than average. For these people, cutting out meat may have more benefits than for someone who is not predisposed to diabetes.

Research in this area has been ongoing since at least the 1930s and has consistently shown that a low-fat, whole-food, plant-based diet can help people not only prevent the development of type 2 diabetes but also manage both types of diabetes. Although the causes of type 1 and type 2 diabetes are different, the end result—the inability of the body to produce or react to insulin—is the same. People with type 1 diabetes cannot control their illness with diet alone; they require regular insulin injections or they will die because their body quickly stops producing any insulin at all. However, for people whose type 2 diabetes is diagnosed early, weight loss and diet may be all they need to manage it because their pancreas is still producing insulin, although their body is becoming resistant to it. According to Oliveira, a study at the Imperial College of London that compared the insulin resistance and muscle fat of vegans and non-vegans found that "plant-eating subjects enjoyed better insulin sensitivity, blood sugar, and insulin levels as well as significantly better pancreatic beta-cell functioning."[11]

Although consuming a lot of fat can increase a person's risk for type 2 diabetes, it is important to remember that not all fats are created equal. Many people think low-fat foods—for example, low-fat flavored yogurt, salad dressing, and cookies—are healthier than the regular version, but in reality, the makers of these foods tend to add extra sugar to compensate for the loss of taste when fat is taken away, which means

Foods that are high in unsaturated fats, such as the ones shown here, are better for a person's health than low-fat processed foods.

they are not actually very healthy. Instead of looking for low-fat processed foods, vegetarians, vegans, and anyone who is trying to eat more healthily should increase their intake of foods that are high in unsaturated fats.

Concern About Cancer

A 2016 report by the CDC ranked cancer as the second leading cause of death for Americans. No matter where it occurs in the body, cancer is a disease of overgrowth. Regular cells grow, divide, and die off. Cancer cells grow and divide, but then the system goes haywire. Cells continue to grow out of control, often intruding into organs and moving to other parts of the body where they continue their out-of-control growth. In 2016, cancer accounted for nearly 30 percent of annual deaths.

Scientists know that many cancers are lifestyle related. The connection between smoking and lung cancer is one example. However, diet is also a leading factor in cancer prevention.

Some people believe a vegetarian or vegan diet can lower cancer rates. According to William Harris, a doctor who maintained a pro-vegetarian website, numerous studies have shown that a vegetarian diet reduces the risk for breast cancer, ovarian cancer, prostate cancer, intestinal cancer, lung cancer, and lymphatic cancer. Harris wrote on his website in 1999, "There are no logical arguments for the continued use of animal source food in the human diet."[12]

However, the American Institute for Cancer Research (AICR) disagrees with this position. According to its website, "It does not appear that vegetarian or vegan diets are any more protective than plant-based diets that include moderate to small amounts of animal foods. AICR recommends that you fill your plate with 2/3 (or more) plant foods and 1/3 (or less) fish, poultry or meat, and dairy."[13] The organization also recommends limiting red meat to 18 ounces or less per week and avoiding processed meats such as sausage, hot dogs, and bacon, as these are high in saturated fat and are made with chemicals that may be linked to cancer.

When researching dietary recommendations, it is important for people to look at the source their information is coming from. For example, a website maintained by one person offers no way for

Is Organic Better?

Many people who turn to a vegetarian or vegan diet to improve their health also consider buying only organic produce. This describes foods that are grown without the use of chemical pesticides or fertilizers, although most organic farmers do use natural versions of these products. A high dose of a natural pesticide can be just as dangerous as a man-made chemical one, but the food that is sold in grocery stores and farmers' markets does not contain enough of any kind of pesticide to hurt consumers. Some people buy organic foods because they have less impact on the earth than other produce; many people also believe that these foods taste better and are healthier. While taste is a personal matter, several studies have found that organic foods have little to no increased health benefits compared to non-organic foods.

Regardless, an increasing number of Americans are seeking out organics. From 1997 to 2017, sales of organic food grew from $3.4 billion to $49.4 billion. Many health-conscious shoppers also seek out natural foods. According to the Mayo Clinic, the terms "organic" and "natural" are not interchangeable, although they are frequently used that way. On a food label, natural "means that it has no artificial colors, flavors or preservatives. It does not refer to the methods or materials used to produce the food ingredients."[1] Some organic foods are also natural, but not all are.

Organic food is more expensive, and not everyone can afford it. Medical professionals and food safety advocates agree that adults and children alike should still eat plenty of fruits and vegetables, and most organizations note that there is no evidence that organic foods have a higher nutritional content than non-organic ones. The Environmental Working Group (EWG) is an organization that is devoted to reducing pesticide levels in the food supply. The EWG, though, firmly states that "All research agrees on the health benefits of a diet that includes fruits and vegetables, and eating fresh produce—organic or conventional, as budget allows—is essential for health."[2]

1. "Organic Foods: Are They Safer? More Nutritious?," Mayo Clinic, April 4, 2018. www.mayoclinic.org/healthy-lifestyle/nutrition-and-healthy-eating/in-depth/organic-food/art-20043880.

2. "EWG's 2019 Shopper's Guide to Pesticides in Produce," Environmental Working Group, March 20, 2019. www.ewg.org/foodnews/summary.php.

readers to verify that person's statements without doing further research on their own. When someone maintains a website solely to convince people of one particular point of view, they often ignore facts about the opposing argument. In much the same way, someone who works for the meat industry and tries to paint vegetarianism as an unhealthy way of life is likely concentrating on their own interests rather than on improving others' health. Any information that does not come from an impartial source should be double checked elsewhere. The AICR and other official medical organizations are the most likely sources of factual information. Also, any website that encourages the visitor to sign up for a newsletter or buy their product in order to take charge of their health should be considered with an especially critical eye; so should information that is more than a few years old, as newer research may have added more clarity or even reversed the previously accepted knowledge on a subject.

A Closer Look

In 2019, *U.S. News & World Report* ranked a Mediterranean diet healthier than a vegetarian diet. While both focus on eating fresh fruits and vegetables, the Mediterranean diet also includes small amounts of fish and poultry.

Food Safety

Aside from improving their health, some vegetarians believe their diet offers further protections, such as reduced exposure to toxic chemicals. According to the Environmental Working Group (EWG), 167 million pounds (75.7 million kg) of pesticides are used on animal feed each year. When animals eat this food, the pesticides get stored in their fat, which means meat and dairy products often contain pesticides, just as produce does. However, there are limits on the amount of pesticides that can be used on fruits and vegetables that are sold at stores. According to toxicologist Carl Winter, who has studied the foods on the EWG's list of plants that have been found to contain the most pesticides, eating those foods "didn't pose a real threat, and substituting the so-called worst ones for organic versions didn't result in any appreciable reduction in risk. 'The actual risk is tiny,' he said."[14] In contrast, because the plants that make up animal feed are not being consumed by humans, they are allowed to be sprayed with higher levels of pesticides. Even

Many people who avoid meat disagree with the practice of keeping livestock confined in small spaces, both because it affects the animals' quality of life and because the close quarters prompt farmers to give the animals antibiotics, which many people do not want in their food.

considering this fact, experts say the levels of pesticides in meat are still not high enough to hurt the people who eat it and point out that all foods sold in stores must pass safety tests. However, many vegetarians and vegans choose to limit their exposure anyway; some do not trust the safety tests because they are done by the companies who sell the meat, so they have a good reason to say their product is safe.

Other concerns for health-conscious eaters are hormones and antibiotics. Livestock are often given hormones to help them grow more muscle or produce more milk, which translates to more product that can be sold at a lower cost. Antibiotics are given to the animals because they live in very close quarters on most farms, which means that if one animal gets sick, it is almost certain that the disease will be passed around to all the other animals. This can ruin the meat or dairy products, and in extreme cases, could result in the livestock dying, which would severely hurt the farm's profits. Consumers worry about hormones and antibiotics in their food because some studies have shown they are harmful to human health, although in most cases the long-term effects remain unknown. None of the evidence has been strong enough for experts to declare a definitive link between these substances and issues such as early-onset puberty or increased cancer risk, but some countries have passed laws limiting or banning the amount of hormones and antibiotics that can be used. In places where these laws do not exist, many people choose to go vegetarian or vegan to avoid the uncertainty of the situation.

Avoiding the problems associated with spoiled or improperly prepared meat is another benefit of vegetarianism. However, vegetarianism does not guarantee complete food safety. A 2018 *E. coli*–infected romaine lettuce outbreak is proof that foodborne pathogens, or germs, can affect vegetarians as well.

Some farmers have cut down trees to make room for more cows, which has affected the environment in negative ways.

Politics and Food

Some people cut out animal products because they are concerned about the effects of livestock farming on both the environment and the animals. As Elisabeth said, "For me, my health and nutrition are no different than the health and nutrition of the planet and the animals that share that planet with me."[15]

Most of America's meats are produced by concentrated animal feeding operations (CAFOs), which are also known as factory farms. CAFOs are extraordinarily efficient at producing cheap meat, but environmentalists, animal activists, and other groups are concerned about the hidden costs to the life and well-being of the animals as well as to humans and the planet.

Greenhouse gases trap the heat coming from the planet's surface similar to the way a greenhouse warms the air inside its glass walls during a cold winter. These gases include water vapor, methane, nitrous oxide, chlorofluorocarbons, and carbon dioxide, and many of these substances contribute to global warming and climate change. Carbon dioxide is the one that is discussed in the media most frequently, but methane causes problems as well. It does not stay in the atmosphere as long as carbon dioxide, but while it is there, it causes global warming much faster than carbon dioxide. Methane can come from man-made sources such as oil and gas production as well as natural sources such as wetlands, melting glaciers, and animal digestion. For instance, when cows burp or pass gas, they are releasing methane. Scientists previously thought methane emissions from cows were not a large problem, but recent research has shown that they produce 11 percent more methane than past studies indicated. When people's consumption of beef and dairy increases, forests are cut down to create grazing room for more cows. This has a double negative effect on global warming: At the same time, carbon-absorbing forests are disappearing and the number of methane-producing cows is increasing.

Factory farms also produce enormous amounts of manure, and getting rid of it can be a problem. According to a 2015 *Newsweek* article, the U.S. Department of Agriculture (USDA) estimates that U.S. livestock produces 335 million tons of manure annually. To dispose of this massive amount of waste, farmers spread manure on fields within and around the farm. In smaller quantities, manure breaks down and is actually good for the soil. However, the large quantity of manure produced by CAFOs means that farmers must pile the waste in deep layers over the fields. The problem is that deep layers of manure cannot break down into the soil. The runoff from the raw manure pollutes nearby streams and waterways with a mix of bacteria, drugs from the animal waste, and ammonia from urine that seeps into the groundwater.

According to author Lierre Keith, some people become vegetarians because they believe it is "honorable, ennobling even. Reasons like justice, compassion, a desperate and all-encompassing longing to set the world right. To save the planet … To protect the vulnerable, the voiceless. To feed the hungry. At the very least to refrain from participating in the horror of factory farming."[16]

However, there are downsides to everything in life, and a meatless diet is no exception. While it is true that reducing the high demand for meat and dairy can have positive effects on the planet, a dramatic increase in the demand for plant-based products would result in different kinds of negative environmental effects, despite claims that being vegetarian or vegan is the most sustainable lifestyle. All people need to eat, so if everyone ate a vegetarian or vegan diet, more food would need to be grown. However, Keith pointed out that "agriculture is the most destructive thing humans have done to the planet, and more of the same won't save us. The truth is that agriculture requires the wholesale destruction of entire ecosystems."[17] Clearing more land for farming could negatively affect the plants and animals that already live in a certain area.

Furthermore, many of the plant-based foods that are in the highest demand must be imported. This requires trucks, boats, and other forms of transportation to run constantly, bringing foods from one country to another. Most of these vehicles run on oil and gas, so increasing the number of vehicles would also increase the amount of fossil fuels leading to global warming and, in turn, climate change. As journalist Emma Henderson noted, "Eating lamb chops that come from a farm a few miles down the road is much better for the environment than eating an avocado that has travelled from the other side of the world."[18]

Furthermore, higher demand for exotic foods has been reportedly harming people in the countries where those foods grow naturally. As more people in the Western world turn to plant-based diets, demand for foods such as avocados and quinoa has skyrocketed, causing shortages that affect non-Westerners. For example, in 2018, Kenya banned the export of avocados because too many were being sent overseas, causing the price to rise in Kenya to a point where many people could not afford them. Mexico was in a similar situation around the same time. Henderson reported,

> Back in December [2017] Mexico was considering importing avocados, which have been a staple in the country for tens of thousands of years. The country's economy secretary, Ildefonso Guajardo, said although Mexico now supplies around 45 per cent of the world's avocados, it wasn't ruling out importing them for their own consumption. And that's because the price per kilo is equivalent to the daily minimum wage, 80 pesos (£3) [$6]. And it's expected to stay at this level too, causing detrimental effects to those for whom this is a staple.[19]

None of this means a vegetarian or vegan diet is bad; instead, the knowledge of these issues has refocused people's attention on buying locally sourced foods from places such as farmers' markets. For people whose main goal in going vegetarian is to help the planet and the people who live on it, these facts may cause them to reconsider whether they want to cut all meat out of their diet.

A Closer Look

In 2018, the *Independent* reported that about 150,000 people participated in "Veganuary," which is when people go vegan for the month of January to test out the diet.

Meat as Murder

The environment is not all vegetarians' main concern. Many cut out meat and other animal products because of their concern for how the animals that provide those items are treated. The strictest vegans object to killing any animal or using anything produced by an animal, including wool, silk, honey, and eggs. Others are focused on how animals are treated before they are killed or the conditions they are kept in while their products are being harvested.

In order to fulfill the huge demand for meat in the United States while keeping costs down and ensuring that a farm makes money, CAFOs keep animals in close confinement for their entire lives, often with little space to move freely or behave naturally. Animal rights activists raise many concerns about the treatment and condition of animals raised to satisfy America's demand for meat. People within the agriculture industry respond that consumer demand drives production methods; the more people demand meat, the more animals farms need to raise to satisfy that demand.

Perhaps the most intensively managed farming involves chickens, raised for both eggs and meat. According to Michael Welch, the former president and CEO of Harrison Poultry, the chicken industry slaughters about 160 million chickens per week to meet consumer demand—a number that has doubled in the last 25 years. In 2015, the HBO show *Last Week Tonight with John Oliver* discussed how chicken farming typically works in the United States. Four large companies—Tyson, Perdue, Sanderson Farms, and Pilgrim's—control the majority of chicken farming. They make contracts with smaller, independent farmers in which the farmers own the equipment needed to raise the chickens and the company owns the chickens themselves. The chickens are delivered

Chickens on modern farms spend most or all of their days in close quarters, with little room to move and no fresh air.

as young chicks and picked up again about a month later, when they are ready to be killed for their meat. Under these contracts, farmers are required to keep the birds crowded in large, windowless barns. One farmer explained that this is because fresh air and sunlight makes the birds more active. Chickens that do nothing but sit and eat all day get fatter, which means more meat for the companies to sell.

Not all food animals endure the harsh living conditions characterized by factory farming operations. Dairy cattle are generally given room to move more freely within barns and corrals. Beef cattle spend time on both rangelands and more crowded feedlots. However, this does not necessarily mean that animal rights activists have no problems or concerns with pasture-farming conditions. There are concerns about the welfare

Animal Exploitation

Many vegans choose not to use any animal products, even those that do not require killing an animal. In many cases, this is because they view it as exploitation, or using an animal unfairly to benefit from them. For example, part of the reason many vegans give up dairy is because they believe it is not right to take milk from cows or goats when their milk is meant to feed their babies. Furthermore, since cows need to give birth in order to produce milk, many people think it is cruel that dairy farmers impregnate their cows every year.

Some people argue that certain animal products are not harmful. For example, some vegans choose not to eat honey because they believe it is exploitative to bees and takes away honey they need to survive the winter. However, many beekeepers say there is an ethical way to harvest honey—by taking only the extra honey and leaving enough to feed the bees. Some beekeepers do take too much, so people who are concerned about this but still want to eat honey should try to buy honey directly from beekeepers and ask questions about their methods.

Wool is another product that has controversy surrounding it. Wild sheep can shed their wool, but domesticated sheep have been bred in such a way that most cannot do this. For this reason, they must be sheared every year; according to the American Society of Animal Science (ASAS), leaving a sheep unshorn can endanger its health and even its life in a number of ways, such as causing it to overheat in the summer. However, many vegans believe shearing is cruel to sheep and have accused sheep shearers of regularly hurting or killing the animals. In 2014, ASAS countered these accusations with a statement that said in part,

> There are established guidelines and educational programs designed to educate farmers and ranchers and to protect sheep … It is not common practice in the sheep industry in the United States or Australia to handle sheep in a violent manner or treat the animals inhumanely … That is not to say that accidental cuts don't occur during the shearing process. These cuts are generally similar to nicks that occur when people are shaving and do not involve serious injury. If the acts are intentional and severe … appropriate corrective action is recommended. Responsible sheep producers care about the animals they are entrusted with.[1]

1. ASAS Board, "There Is No Such Thing as Humane Wool When It Is Left on the Sheep: Why Sheep Shearing Is Absolutely Necessary for Sheep Welfare," ASAS, July 14, 2014. www.asas.org/taking-stock/blog-post/taking-stock/2014/07/14/there-is-no-such-thing-as-humane-wool-when-it-is-left-on-the-sheep-why-sheep-shearing-is-absolutely-necessary-for-sheep-welfare.

of cattle and other livestock during their transport to slaughterhouses as well as the methods for killing them and processing them into food.

Pigs, sheep, and cattle are transported from farms and feedlots to the slaughterhouse on tightly packed, non-climate controlled transport trucks or railcars. During transport, the animals may be subjected to temperature extremes and lack food and water, often for more than 24 hours. Animal rights groups claim that many animals are injured or die during transport due to trampling, freezing, or dehydration.

Once at the slaughterhouse, animals are supposed to be killed according to the guidelines outlined in the Humane Slaughter Act, a law enacted in 1958 to minimize the suffering of animals killed for food. The law requires cattle, hogs, sheep, and horses to be made unconscious by a blow to the head with a stun gun or electric shock prior to slaughter so they are not able to feel pain. However, animal rights organizations claim—and the farming industry acknowledges—that proper stunning does not always take place.

One reason slaughterhouses give for why they violate the Humane Slaughter Act is the rate at which animals are processed. In some factories, more than 300 animals go down the production line each hour. At these large factories, cattle are stunned and hoisted onto an overhead chain within 12 seconds of entering the killing chamber. This rate provides workers little time to accurately stun the animals, forcing them to send the animals down the line even if they are still conscious. If the initial stunning attempt does not properly render the animal unconscious, there is no time to make another attempt before the next animal comes down the line, so they need to keep moving.

By reducing or ending their meat consumption, many people hope to improve the conditions for farm animals by reducing the overall demand for meat. However, even those who continue to eat meat can—and do—campaign for better treatment of animals on CAFOs. Animal science experts who work in the meat industry continue to seek ways to improve the slaughtering process in an effort to enhance animal welfare and slaughter the animals as humanely as possible. Dr. Temple Grandin, an animal sciences professor at Colorado State University, advises slaughterhouses on ways to design facilities and handle animals that would minimize fear and ensure that animals are killed humanely. She also points out that humane slaughter is much more likely when meat buyers monitor the factories. Some food companies conduct audits of factories and will not buy meat from facilities where abuses are recorded.

Many consumers have also balanced their desire to continue eating animal products with their wish to see animals treated well by choosing to buy from local farms, where they can meet the farmers and see for themselves that the animals are taken care of while they are alive as well as being slaughtered humanely. In addition, farm-to-table restaurants have grown in popularity. These are restaurants that commit to serving only locally produced, ethically sourced food. They work directly with farmers, ranchers, and fishers to ensure that the practices of the facility are humane and that the animals are all raised and slaughtered in the immediate area. They also follow quotas set by the government to prevent overfishing. Food in this type of restaurant is generally much more expensive than at a traditional restaurant that gets its meat from large suppliers. However, this is because the quality of the food is better and the farms are raising fewer animals to give them more space while they are alive. Many people like farm-to-table restaurants because they are better for the environment; for the animals that are raised for their meat; and for people's health, since the food is often guaranteed to be fresh and contain no antibiotics or artificial hormones.

In the end, each person must decide what is right for themselves. There are compelling reasons to abstain from meat consumption, but even reducing the amount of meat a person eats, rather than eliminating it completely, can have a positive impact on both individual health and the environment.

As concern for animal welfare has grown in the 21st century, businesses have been created to provide consumers with products from farms that treat their animals well.

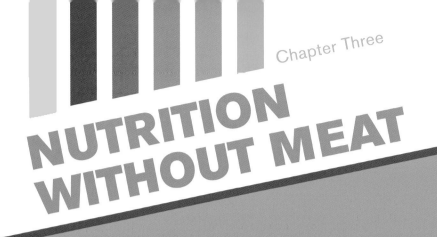

Chapter Three

NUTRITION WITHOUT MEAT

Lean meat is a good source of protein, and people who cut it out of their diet must be sure to replace it with enough plant sources of protein to stay healthy. This can be challenging for some vegetarians and vegans; proper nutrition is a bit more complicated than simply eating anything that is not an animal product.

A Ratio for Health

Like the standard American diet, the vegetarian and vegan diets have food pyramids. Each pyramid provides a visual clue about how to eat. The top, pointed section is the smallest portion and is for fats, oils, and sweets. The pyramid suggests these be used sparingly. A single serving of fats, oils or sweets would equal one teaspoon of oil or butter, one teaspoon of sugar, one teaspoon of honey, or one tablespoon of mayonnaise or salad dressing. This section also includes sources of healthy fats, such as avocados and nuts, but these should still be eaten relatively sparingly.

In the next section of the vegetarian pyramid sit dairy and protein. Dairy is an excellent source of calcium, which is essential for building strong bones and teeth as well as for helping blood clot after an injury and allowing muscles—including the heart—to contract properly. Both calcium and protein are essential for human health, and two to three servings of each are recommended each day. A single serving of dairy would include 1 cup of milk or soy milk, 1 cup of yogurt, or 1.5 ounces (45 g) of cheese. A single serving of protein would include half a cup of cooked beans, 4 ounces (115 g) of tofu, 1 egg, or 2 tablespoons of nuts, seeds, or peanut butter.

Meat is loaded with protein. It is important for vegetarians and vegans to get protein from other foods, such as some of the ones shown here.

Fruits and vegetables make up the next section. Three to five servings of vegetables are recommended daily. In fact, some nutritionists are now saying Americans should have up to nine servings of vegetables a day. A single serving of vegetables would be one cup raw or half a cup cooked.

Because of their sugar content, the recommendation is for fewer fruits than vegetables, but two to four servings is consistent with a healthy diet. A single serving would be one piece of fresh fruit, half a cup of sliced or chopped fruit, a quarter cup of dried fruit, or three-quarters of a cup of fruit juice. Choosing a variety of fruits is important because each fruit offers different benefits. For example, citrus fruit is high in vitamin C, berries provide antioxidants, and bananas are rich in potassium. By choosing a variety of textures and colors, people will consume a variety of nutrients.

Breads, cereals, and pastas make up the largest group, with six or more servings being recommended. White flour, rice, and sugar are discouraged; these all offer empty calories, raise blood sugar too quickly, and offer little to no nutritional benefits. Better choices include whole wheat breads, brown rice and other whole grains, and whole wheat pasta. For vegans, this section may be a bit tricky because many grain foods also contain eggs or milk. When buying food from a supermarket, vegans should be sure to read all the ingredients on a package to make sure none of the foods they are trying to avoid are in there.

Six servings of grain may sound like a lot, but servings can add up fast. A single serving would include one slice of bread, one-fourth of a bagel, half of an English muffin, or three-fourths of a cup of cereal.

All of this information can sound overwhelming. On her website, Vegan Coach, nutritional consultant Patty Knutson wrote, "When most of us first go vegan, we sort of wing it because we usually have ZERO clue about what we're doing … It happened to me too. Things went along just fine for a while, but then I started to realize I was getting sort of tired. Like, a lot!"[20] After studying the vegan pyramid and using its guidelines to change her diet, Knutson found that she had more energy and felt better because she was getting the proper nutrients.

However, Knutson and other experts stress that the pyramid does not have to be followed perfectly every day in order to keep someone healthy. The website Nutriciously explained that there is "no need to stress over eating a 'perfect diet' and following these recommendations all of the time—it's what you put on your plate most days [that] matters. If you don't feel like eating all of the suggested serving sizes each day or you don't have access to these foods, it's not a big deal. Most likely, it will balance out over the course of a few days."[21]

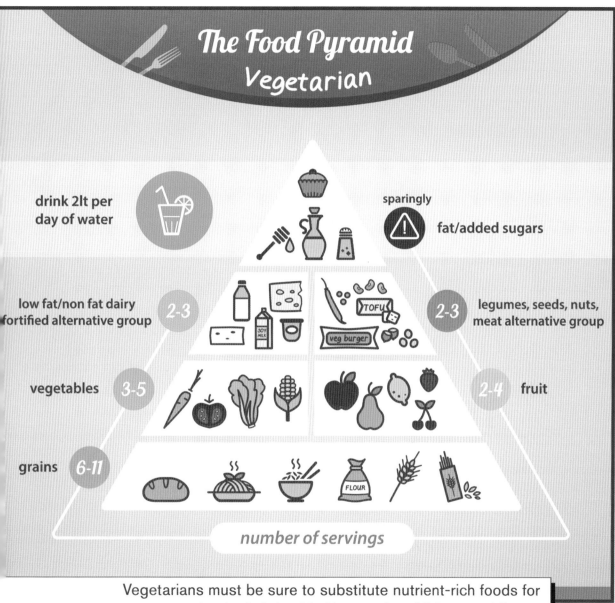

The Food Pyramid
Vegetarian

drink 2lt per day of water

sparingly
fat/added sugars

low fat/non fat dairy fortified alternative group — 2-3

legumes, seeds, nuts, meat alternative group — 2-3

vegetables — 3-5

fruit — 2-4

grains — 6-11

number of servings

Vegetarians must be sure to substitute nutrient-rich foods for meat to maintain their health. Vegans, in addition to adding meat substitutes to their diet, must add dairy substitutes.

Nuts provide a lot of protein and many vitamins and minerals.

A Varied Diet

A varied diet is key to a healthy lifestyle for anyone, but it is essential for a vegetarian or vegan, especially one who is young. Because children and teens are growing so rapidly, they are especially vulnerable to nutritional deficiencies if they have poor eating habits, so an assortment of healthy foods is important for them.

Christina Economos, a nutrition professor, directed the Tufts University Longitudinal Health Study on the lifestyle habits of young adults. In 2002, *TIME* magazine reported that her research indicated that

> *kids who were most influenced by family diet and health values are eating healthy vegetarian or low-meat diets. But there is a whole*

group of students who decide to become vegetarians and do it in a poor way ... They eat more bread, cheese, and pastry products and load up on salad dressing. Their saturated-fat intake is no lower than red-meat eaters, and they are more likely to consume inadequate amounts of vitamin B12 and protein. They may think they are healthier because they are some sort of vegetarian and they don't eat red meat, but in fact they may be less healthy.[22]

Matt, one of the college students who participated in the Tufts study, confirmed these results. He said, "I was lazy, I know that now. I wanted to go veg, but I didn't want to cook. So, I lived on potato tacos and blue Slurpees. It didn't take long before I felt awful. 'But hey,' I thought, 'it can't be my diet—after all, I'm a vegetarian!'"[23] Rather than fried food and sweet,

Potato chips are vegetarian, but they are not healthy.

carbonated beverages, a healthy diet—whether it includes animal products or not—contains all the major nutrients needed to build a strong body.

Understanding Nutrients

Carbohydrates are the fuels that run the human engine. They come in two forms. Simple carbohydrates tend to be white; these break down quickly in the body, giving a quick "high" followed by a drop in energy. Complex carbohydrates—including whole grains—are more likely to be brown. They have fiber in them and take longer to break down. These carbohydrates provide energy for a longer period of time and also provide a sustained feeling of fullness due to their higher fiber content.

Proteins are a major component of all living cells and are needed for growth and repair of tissue as well as proper functioning of the organs. In addition to animal products, proteins are found in legumes, nuts, soy, and many other foods. Tofu, which is made from soybeans and is a staple of many vegetarians' and vegans' diets, is an excellent source of protein.

A Closer Look

According to a 2017 article from *Business Insider*, a large order of Five Guys french fries contains 1,314 calories and more fat than six Krispy Kreme donuts.

Proteins are made up of amino acids, and there are 20 different kinds of these. Nine of them are known as essential amino acids because they are not made by the human body naturally. The best sources of protein are called complete proteins because they contain good amounts of all nine essential amino acids. Cheese, eggs, fish, meat, and milk are all complete proteins. Grains, legumes, nuts, and vegetables are all called incomplete proteins because, while they provide some essential amino acids, not all nine are present in these foods. However, this does not mean animal products are better than plant products or essential for good health because combining two or more incomplete proteins can provide the proper amount of essential amino acids in one meal. What is important is having a varied diet and eating enough vegetables, nuts, and whole grains to get the required amount of each amino acid.

Good fats are essential to human health because they lower cholesterol, protect against heart disease, support healthy skin, develop body cells, and protect against cancer. Good fats are found in nuts, olives, avocados, and seeds. Although necessary, fats should be eaten sparingly.

Vitamins and minerals are the building blocks of the body. The majority of these nutrients are easy to get through a vegetarian diet. Whole grains, legumes, and leafy greens are the heroes of the group, packing vitamins and minerals in almost every category. Richly colored fruits and vegetables round out the diet while providing a healthy dose of vital nutrients.

Adding Nutrients

It may seem difficult to consistently get all the recommended servings of various foods, but there are a few simple ways to add more healthy foods, especially fruits and vegetables, to any diet while decreasing meat consumption at the same time. These include:

- adding vegetables to pasta sauce
- serving smaller portions of the main dish and adding a side salad
- having fruit for dessert instead of sweets
- eating pasta made from vegetables
- adding blueberries or bananas to cereal
- snacking on carrot sticks or dried fruit
- substituting tofu for a meat product—for example, adding tofu to pasta instead of chicken
- drinking 100 percent fruit juice or smoothies with little to no added sugar
- putting vegetables on pizza
- eating fresh vegetables instead of chips with dip
- making baked banana or zucchini chips to substitute for fried potato chips
- replacing one serving of grains per day with a fruit or vegetable—for example, making a wrap with lettuce instead of a tortilla

Iron, Calcium, and B12

Certain nutrients are more difficult for vegetarians to obtain. Without meat, vegetarians have to work a little harder to get their iron needs met. This is especially important for people who have periods because each month, they lose iron when they bleed, and that iron must be replaced. The recommended daily allowance of iron for children is 10 milligrams, and for teens it is between 11 and 15 milligrams, depending on their sex and level of physical activity. For adults who do not have periods, including women over the age of 50, it is 8 milligrams, but adults who do have periods need more than double that amount—18 milligrams each day. Good sources of plant-based iron include kidney beans, oatmeal, cooked spinach, and tofu.

Someone does not have to eat meat to get their recommended daily amount of iron. There are many good plant-based sources of iron, as this photo shows.

Plant-based iron is generally harder to digest than animal-based iron, but if plant-based iron is combined with vitamin C, it may be easier for the body to absorb. For example, a spinach salad tossed with some cranberries or orange slices will provide a healthy dose of both iron and vitamin C. Other sources of iron include dried beans; dried fruit such as prunes, raisins, and figs; molasses; dark leafy greens; and cocoa.

A Closer Look

With a little planning, it is possible to get enough nutrients from plants only. In 2003, the American Dietetic Association and the Dietitians of Canada reported that vegetarians and vegans who follow a healthy diet actually tend to get more iron than meat-eaters.

Most vegetarians can easily get calcium from dairy products such as cheese and milk, but vegans need to work a little harder. Adults need 1,000 milligrams of calcium daily. Children, teens, pregnant people, people who are breastfeeding, women over 50, and men over 70 have higher needs for calcium—up to 1,300 milligrams per day. Vegans can fulfill their calcium needs by eating foods such as spinach, kale, broccoli, white beans, and almonds as well as dairy substitutes that have been fortified with calcium, meaning they have had calcium added to them. One example is tofu. It naturally contains about 100 milligrams of calcium per three-quarter cup serving, but when calcium is added, that number can rise to more than 800 milligrams. In comparison, a cup of low-fat milk contains about 305 milligrams of calcium. Maintaining good calcium intake is especially important for young people because the teen years are a time of significant bone building. Having enough calcium in the diet can decrease their risk of developing osteoporosis—a disease that makes bones break more easily—when they are older.

Other vitamins and minerals may also be hard to come by when following a strict vegetarian or vegan diet. It is always best for someone to check with a licensed medical professional before they dramatically change their eating habits.

A Variety of Vegetarians

The ways in which a person meets their dietary needs will vary depending on what kind of vegetarian or vegan diet they follow. For people who eat no meat, poultry, or fish at all, filling out their diet with a variety of plant-based foods is essential.

Lacto-ovo is the most common type of vegetarian diet in the United States. It is also what people generally think of when they think of vegetarians. Lacto-ovo vegetarians eat dairy and eggs in addition to a plant-based diet. This diet is the easiest to follow when eating out, since many restaurants have meat-free options. Additionally, a dish such as pasta with chicken can easily be ordered without the meat, giving vegetarians a lot of flexibility with menu items.

As with all vegetarian diets, plant-based foods need to be the emphasis. If a person loads up on too many eggs and dairy products and consumes too much fat, it is possible they will face the same weight and health challenges as a non-vegetarian. By following the food pyramid guidelines, lacto-ovo vegetarians can enjoy a healthy diet and avoid overconsumption.

The lacto vegetarian diet requires a bit more work, since many foods contain eggs; for example, mayonnaise is made from eggs, so they must be careful when ordering a sandwich at a restaurant to ask about all the ingredients. However, it is still relatively easy to follow, especially if someone does most of their own cooking. Lacto vegetarians can easily obtain the calcium they need through milk, cheese, and yogurt. Protein needs, too, are easily met through either dairy products or plant-based protein sources. However, as with lacto-ovo vegetarians, too much fat can be a risk if lacto vegetarians do not monitor their dairy and sugar intake: A cheese pizza and chocolate milkshake is a lacto vegetarian meal, but not a healthy one. Like any vegetarian, it is important for lacto vegetarians to eat a wide variety of foods to ensure that they meet all their nutrient needs.

A Closer Look

According to the Bureau of Labor Statistics, demand for dieticians and nutritionists is projected to grow 15 percent between 2016 and 2026.

Most types of pasta are fine for lacto vegetarians to eat, but egg noodles (shown here) are made with eggs. Reading labels carefully is important for anyone with a special diet.

Ovo vegetarians eat eggs but do not use milk products. For this reason, they must find a way to add calcium to their diet. Soy, rice, and almond milk products are on the market and are often fortified with both calcium and vitamin D. Any of these products can be substituted for cow's milk for drinking and in most recipes.

For people who have increased calcium needs, calcium-fortified foods are helpful. Many cereals, juices, soy products, and other foods are now fortified with calcium. Some have both calcium and added vitamin D. Other sources of calcium include leafy greens, broccoli, seaweed, and sesame seeds.

For some time, health professionals discouraged people from eating eggs because the yolk contains 210 milligrams of cholesterol. However, new research has shown that eggs do not raise cholesterol levels in most people. In fact, a 2018 study from the University of Sydney in Australia found that eating two eggs a day, six days a week was safe even for people with type 2 diabetes. Cholesterol levels in participants did not rise, and many reported feeling full and eating less throughout the day after consuming the eggs.

Looking at Veganism

Vegans eat only plant-based foods and avoid both dairy and eggs. Many vegans do not eat honey because they view this as "stealing" from honeybees. Generally, they also do not wear leather. Some do not wear wool or silk either, as these also come from animals, but others do because, unlike with leather, the sheep and worms that produce these materials are not killed when humans harvest them. They are also careful not to buy any products with animal-derived ingredients. This can be very challenging because many food items contain at least some animal products. For example, gelatin comes from animals, so gummy candy and marshmallows are generally off-limits. So is milk chocolate, because of the added milk; non-dairy creamer, which often adds a small amount of a milk protein called calcium caseinate; red foods, which are often colored with a dye made from an insect called the cochineal; veggie burgers, which may contain eggs; and Worcestershire sauce, which is made with a type of fish called an anchovy. Some vegans are less strict than others and will choose to eat some of these foods, especially if vegan substitutes are not readily available, but many are fully committed to the lifestyle and make sure to read all the ingredients on the items they buy.

A Closer Look

There are more than 30 synonyms for dairy that vegans need to be aware of when they are looking at packaged foods. Some are easily identifiable, such as cheese and butter, but others are less well-known. These include casein, half and half, curds, whey, lactose, nougat, and ghee.

It only takes one ingredient to make a food non-vegetarian or non-vegan. Anchovies (shown here) are the only ingredient in Worcestershire sauce that is not vegan.

Without nutrient-dense egg and dairy products, it can be difficult for vegans to get all the vitamins and minerals they need. Big plates of fiber-rich foods can fill a stomach before the body obtains all the nutrients it needs. If the empty calories in sweets and sodas are added to the mix, it can be impossible to fulfill nutritional needs.

Like vegetarians, most vegans add soy to their diet because it is a complete protein, is rich in calcium, iron, and folate, and contains complex carbohydrates as well as the healthy fat omega-3. Common soy foods include tofu and soy milk. Whole soybeans in the pod, known as edamame, are now widely available in U.S. grocery stores. Soy protein is also used to

When Diet Becomes a Problem

The majority of vegans and vegetarians eat healthily and choose their lifestyle because of various health, environmental, or animal welfare concerns. However, some people use it as a way to hide an eating disorder. These include anorexia, which is characterized by severely—and dangerously—restricting food intake, and bulimia, which involves periods of eating a large amount of food (bingeing) followed by finding a way to quickly expel it from the body before it gets digested (purging). One eating disorder that has become more common since healthy eating started being promoted in the media is called orthorexia. This involves taking a healthy diet to such an extreme that it becomes unhealthy. Registered dietician Abby Sharp explained, "While my orthorexia was largely based around a fear of sugar, for others that could be fat, gluten, or in this case, animal products."[1]

In an article for the *Daily Beast*, Danielle Friedman wrote about Jill Miller, who used veganism to cover up her eating disorders. Miller "turned down food with the seemingly innocent, even noble excuse that no one could argue with: Oh, sorry. I can't eat that—I'm vegan … [Miller explained,] 'It was a convenient way to eliminate fat and calories.'"[2] Miller eventually started eating animal products again as part of her journey to take back control from her eating disorders.

Vegetarianism and veganism are not eating disorders in and of themselves, and someone does not have to give them up in order to have a healthy diet or a healthy mentality. However, some signs that a person is using one of these diets as a way to hide a disorder include:

- They feel disgusted with themselves when they eat.
- They are not eating enough calories to meet their body's needs.
- They binge and purge.
- They give up meat or other animal products solely to lose weight, even if they were not overweight to begin with.
- They eliminate foods from their diet without replacing them with different foods.
- Preoccupation with following their self-imposed dietary rules stops them from enjoying activities.
- They have an obsession with eating only healthy foods.

1. Quoted in Jessica Brown, "The Dark Side of Veganism: How the Diet Can Be a Cover for Disordered Eating," *Independent*, September 17, 2018. www.independent.co.uk/news/long_reads/veganism-orthorexia-dieting-anorexia-food-bloggers-diet-vegans-a8537211.html.

2. Quoted in Danielle Friedman, "When Veganism Is an Eating Disorder," *Daily Beast*, July 14, 2017. www.thedailybeast.com/when-veganism-is-an-eating-disorder.

make a number of meat substitutes. Soy burgers, soy hot dogs, soy "chicken," soy cheese, and soy yogurts are just a few of the products available in American grocery stores. Additionally, many soy products are supplemented with essential vitamins and minerals that may be difficult for vegans and vegetarians to otherwise get in their diet.

Vegans must also supplement their diets with vitamin B12 because it is found almost exclusively in animal products, although a few plants, such as mushrooms, do contain small amounts. Stephen Walsh of the Vegan Society explained:

> *Most vegans consume enough B12 to avoid anemia and nervous system damage, but many do not get enough to minimize potential risk of heart disease or pregnancy complications. To get the full benefit of a vegan diet, vegans should do one of the following:*
>
> *1. Eat fortified foods two or three times a day to get at least three micrograms … of B12 a day*
> *2. OR Take one B12 supplement daily providing at least 10 micrograms*
> *3. OR Take a weekly B12 supplement providing at least 2000 micrograms.*
>
> *If relying on fortified foods, check the labels carefully to make sure you are getting enough B12. For example, if a fortified plant milk contains 1 microgram of B12 per serving then consuming three servings a day will provide adequate vitamin B12. Others may find the use of B12 supplements more convenient and economical.*[24]

Symptoms of B12 deficiency include loss of energy, tingling and numbness in the limbs, blurred vision, sore tongue, confusion, hallucinations, and personality changes. Someone may have all of these symptoms or only a few. A blood test can check whether someone's levels of B12 are high enough, but Walsh warned, "A blood B12 level measurement is a very unreliable test for vegans, particularly for vegans using any form of algae [as a supplement]."[25] Algae and certain other plants contain false B12, which can make it seem as though someone's blood levels are higher than they actually are. Methylmalonic acid (MMA) testing, Walsh said, is the best test to determine vegans' levels of B12.

Shown here are common sources of vitamin B12. Vegans must eat fortified foods or take a B12 supplement to make sure they are getting enough of this nutrient.

Vitamin D, which can be obtained from fortified cow's milk, is another nutrient that is difficult for vegans to acquire through food. However, it is also the only vitamin that humans do not have to get from food. The body can process vitamin D from sunshine, so a 15-minute walk during a sunny day will provide all the vitamin D someone needs. For people who live in places without much sunshine, taking a supplement is also a good idea.

Iron and calcium can also be tricky nutrients for vegans. Vegans must pay attention to be sure they are including fortified cereals and milks as well as a variety of nutrient-rich vegetables in their diets. The recommendations for vegetarians about these nutrients apply to vegans as well.

Chapter Four

A CROSS-CULTURAL PHENOMENON

The American diet has influenced virtually every nation in the world. This often has negative effects. Modern American food can be highly processed and contain high levels of saturated fat and refined sugars. As these foods have entered the international market, many populations that have historically eaten largely plant-based diets are now seeing an increase in obesity, cancer, and heart disease. These are the same health problems that lead many Americans to explore vegetarianism.

Holy Cows

By far, the country with the most vegetarians—nearly 38 percent of the population, according to government surveys—is India. However, in 2018, the BBC reported on research by U.S.-based anthropologist Balmurli Natrajan and India-based economist Suraj Jacob that suggested these results are inaccurate. Their research shows that only about 20 percent of Indians are truly vegetarian; the rest "under-report eating meat—particularly beef—and over-report eating vegetarian food."[26] The main reason for this is political and cultural pressure that is deeply ingrained in India's history. In India, vegetarianism is tied to historic religious beliefs. About 80 percent of Indians are Hindu. Hinduism does not have a single holy book or one particular deity. Instead, Hindus may worship any of thousands of gods and goddesses. Those deities are thought to be the manifestation of Brahma, or the supreme soul.

Hindus believe that all souls reincarnate until they eventually reunite with Brahma. Depending on a soul's karma—the consequences of one's actions—a soul may be born into a higher or lower station. It will reincarnate until it eventually joins Brahma and finds release from the cycle of birth, death, and rebirth. Because Hindus believe that divinity inhabits all living beings, including humans and animals, they practice ahimsa, or nonviolence toward all living creatures. This belief in ahimsa is the basis for vegetarianism in the Hindu religion. They also believe cows are holy and need to be protected, which is why they oppose even non-Hindus eating beef. The BBC reported that a political party in India called the Bharatiya Janata Party (BJP) promotes Hindu beliefs and vegetarianism. Since Narendra Modi, the BJP-affiliated prime minister, took power, "vigilante cow protection groups, operating with impunity [freedom from punishment], have killed people transporting cattle."[27]

Despite this pressure, many Indians continue to eat meat, although it is still viewed as a largely vegetarian country. For example, the city of Chennai is thought of as a place where most meals are vegetarian,

India is a large country, and Indian food varies from region to region. However, thanks partially to migration, multiple vegetarian dishes can be found in any region.

but only about 6 percent of the city actually eats vegetarian consistently. According to Natrajan and Jacob, there are several reasons for this misconception. One is that, in a "highly diverse society with food habits and cuisines changing every few kilometres and within social groups, any generalisation about large segments of the population is a function of who speaks for the group. This power to represent communities, regions, or even the entire country is what makes the stereotypes."[28] Another reason is migration; when "south Indians migrate to northern and central India, their food comes to stand in for all south Indian cuisine. This is similarly true for north Indians who migrate to other parts of the country."[29] People who meet one or two vegetarians may then conclude that everyone from that part of the country is vegetarian.

A Closer Look

During the Catholic season of Lent, people abstain from meat on Fridays as a way to draw closer to God. However, according to Michael Foley, associate professor at Baylor University and author of the book *Why Do Catholics Eat Fish on Friday?*, only warm-blooded animals are part of the ban. Cold-blooded animals, including fish, snakes, and alligators, are all technically allowed by the religion.

As the country becomes more developed, many people are moving away from traditional beliefs on eating and lifestyle. As they do, Indians are engaging in other habits that negatively affect their health. For example, many rural young men now smoke. Coffee or tea is consumed by the majority of people who live in cities, and 13 percent of Indians drink alcohol. Urban jobs, while offering wages previously unheard of in India, are also inflicting enormous stress on workers. As Indians rapidly change their lifestyles, old health problems clash with new ones to create a difficult path for the country. Today, diseases of extreme poverty such as malaria and malnutrition exist next to diseases of wealth, such as diabetes and hypertension (high blood pressure).

Changing Tastes

Like food patterns in America, typical foods in India vary from region to region. Grains and legumes (especially red lentils) are both diet staples. Areas in the north generally use milk and yogurt products. Eastern areas rely more on fish and rice. Spices such as cardamom, chili pepper, cumin, saffron, and turmeric are common throughout the country.

While some Indians are eating more like Americans, many Americans are eating more Indian food. In America, Indian restaurants are common in many urban areas. According to the Office of the United States Trade Representative, the United States imported $2.7 billion worth of agricultural products from India in 2018. Spices, rice, cooking oils, processed fruit, and vegetables were the most common imports. Curries, lentils, and chai tea are all becoming commonplace choices. Indian products are found in restaurants and supermarkets alike. Those new products reflect the growing interest in both multicultural and healthy food choices in the United States.

The Healthiest Region in the World?

The Mediterranean diet has been gaining attention since the 1990s. By that time, scientists at Harvard School of Public Health, the World Health Organization, and the nonprofit group Oldways noticed that this diet produced remarkable health results. Chronic disease rates around the Mediterranean Sea were some of the lowest in the world, and life expectancies were among the highest, even though medical services in the area were limited.

As they studied eating habits in the region, these scientists found several characteristics in common. An abundance of plant-based foods such as fruits, vegetables, nuts, cereals, and breads are the diet's base. Red meat is used sparingly, dairy use is low, and fish intake is moderate. The limited amounts of dairy products are generally fermented to create yogurt and cheese, with feta being the most commonly eaten cheese. Eggs are consumed no more than four times a week. Wine is drunk in moderate amounts, and olive oil is the major source of oil and fat. Legumes such as black beans, lentils, and garbanzo beans are frequently eaten. Fruit, especially fresh fruit, is often eaten as a snack or dessert,

Fruits, vegetables, whole grains, and healthy fats are staples of the Mediterranean diet.

with honey rather than processed sugar as an accompaniment. Unlike the American diet, the Mediterranean diet typically consists strictly of the three daily meals; snacking during the day is uncommon, and the snacks people do consume tend to be healthy, such as a bowl of fruit. Finally, the people in this region tend to be very physically active.

Because dairy products and meat are used as condiments—added for flavoring and not a main component of the diet—vegetarians can easily adapt this diet to their needs. With its rich mix of vegetables, grains, and legumes, requirements for vitamins and protein are easily met even when the meat has been removed.

The Mediterranean diet is not a single diet. It is a mix of diets from cultures around the Mediterranean Sea. It is also not a strictly vegetarian diet. However, many vegetarians and non-vegetarians alike embrace portions of this diet for its healthful, whole-foods approach to eating. With its emphasis on keeping foods as natural and unprocessed as possible, the diet is rich in fiber and healthy antioxidants.

In 2019, the American Heart Association advised that the Mediterranean diet may be useful for the prevention and treatment of cardiovascular disease. Olive oil, which is a healthy fat, is the main dietary fat in the Mediterranean diet. It is high in monounsaturated fatty acids, which are known to reduce blood pressure and lower cholesterol. Its antioxidants help prevent clogged arteries and lower the risk of cancer.

Regardless of diet, exercise is an important part of a healthy lifestyle.

A European study published in the *New England Journal of Medicine* followed 22,000 people practicing the diet for four years. The closer people stayed to the diet, the less likely they were to die of either heart disease or cancer.

The Land of the Rising Sun

For centuries, the Japanese diet has been considered one of the healthiest in the world. The people of Okinawa in particular have been the subject of many studies and have inspired scientists with their vibrant health; many people live to be at least 100. Although scientists believe up to 50 percent of the Okinawans' long life can be attributed to good genes, they say diet may make up the other half.

A history book titled *Gishi-wajin-den* that was written in the third century BC detailed the beginnings of the traditional Japanese diet: "There are no cattle, no horses, no tigers, no leopards, no goats and no magpies in that land. The climate is mild and people over there eat fresh vegetables both in summer and in winter."[30]

The traditional Japanese diet began to change in the last half of the 20th century. After World War II, many Japanese adopted Americans' eating patterns, and a serious increase in disease followed. When eating a traditional diet, only 1 percent of Japanese were obese, and only 1 to 5 percent of those over 40 years old suffered from diabetes. However, when they began eating a Westernized diet, diabetes rates shot up to 11 to 12 percent, and obesity climbed toward an average of 30 percent.

The increase in disease made scientists take a closer look at the Japanese diet. Good genes aside, they wanted to find out why the Okinawans lived so long. Several factors stood out, including calorie restriction, nutrients, and antioxidants.

Unlike whole grains (shown here), processed grains spike blood sugar levels and can cause digestive problems.

Calorie restriction is one of the main reasons the Okinawans live so long. Okinawans eat 25 percent fewer calories than other Japanese. However, the high levels of nutrients and antioxidants in the food they do eat may also contribute to the low rates of dementia—a degenerative disease that affects a person's memory—cardiovascular disease, and cancer among Okinawans. They get their nutrients from numerous different sources.

One source is cruciferous vegetables. Okinawans consume five times the amount of cabbage, broccoli, brussels sprouts, kale, cauliflower, radishes, watercress, and parsnips that Americans eat. Another dietary source is shiitake mushrooms. Used as a medicine for more than 6,000 years, these mushrooms are loaded with powerful antioxidants and are known for their ability to enhance the immune system and lower cholesterol. Seaweed is high in iodine and minerals and is a regular part of the Okinawan diet.

Tofu, a staple of the Japanese diet, has been shown to lower cholesterol and improve cardiovascular function. It is a good source of protein and is packed with nutrients. Green tea, another staple, has been linked to reduced cancer risk. Green tea has also been shown to lower blood pressure and cholesterol and decrease the risk of stroke and heart disease. Lastly, the Japanese consume more than 154 pounds (70 kg) of fish per person per year. Fish is rich in essential fatty acids that contribute to good health. Some people have criticized Japan for overfishing to meet this demand, but others note that demand for fish is not uniquely Japanese. Regardless, many vegans and vegetarians are campaigning to get people to reduce or eliminate their fish intake to protect declining fish populations.

Matcha (shown here) is a type of green tea that has cultural significance in Japan. It is even healthier than regular green tea because it is grown in a way that gives it more antioxidants. Additionally, the leaves are ground into a powder and dissolved in hot water, so drinkers end up consuming the whole leaf and therefore more of the nutrients.

Americans have been increasingly drawn to the Japanese diet. Rice vinegar sales have increased significantly, and green tea sales have skyrocketed. In 2016, Japan exported an all-time high of almost 10,000 tons of Japanese rice. This was a 31 percent increase from the previous year. Due to high demand for Japanese cooking, the Culinary Institute of America developed an Advanced Cooking of Japanese Cuisine course in 2017.

Small modifications can make the Japanese diet a healthy choice for vegetarians and vegans. Replacing fish with tofu or tempeh, another soy product, is an easy alteration. Rice, seaweed, and fruits and vegetables common to the cuisine provide varied and healthy options.

A Bad Influence

Like the Japanese diet, the traditional Chinese diet, which is built on grains, vegetables, and legumes, is easily adapted to a vegetarian diet. Chinese cuisine includes generous amounts of dark leafy greens, including romaine lettuce, watercress, bok choy (white-stemmed cabbage), kai choy (mustard cabbage), and Chinese kale.

However, as China develops a modern economy, its consumption of meat is skyrocketing. More than half of all Chinese come from low-income and rural households that get more than three-fourths of their calories from grains, and meat has always been an infrequent luxury to a large segment of the population. Today, however, nearly 7.7 pounds (3.5 kg) of poultry are eaten annually even in the poorest households. In comparison, the average American eats 93.6 pounds (41.1 kg) of poultry annually.

As China's economy rapidly changes, people in the middle and upper classes are changing their diets. China's beef consumption has increased from 3.5 million tons in 1996 to 7.3 million tons in 2015—a 111 percent increase over 20 years. Much of that beef is eaten at fast food restaurants or is purchased from Western-style supermarkets. As in many nations, America's economy and customs represent a model to be copied in China, and meat consumption is a hallmark of America's relative luxury. As their diet changes, however, so do rates of diet-related diseases, which have increased over the years.

Americans, on the other hand, are asking for authentic Chinese food and adapting recipes to include healthy choices in their diets. Chinese restaurants have been in America for more than 100 years, but the Chinese food served in America looks nothing like native Chinese food. Americanized Chinese food has more fat, more meat, and more syrupy sauces than authentic Chinese food. However, as Americans seek healthier food choices, they are beginning to look for more authentic Chinese ingredients.

A Closer Look

In 2017, CNN reported that there are more than 41,000 Chinese restaurants in the United States.

Stir-fry vegetables are available pre-chopped and packaged in most produce sections, and bags of mixed bok choy, snow peas, and broccoli can be found in the frozen food sections of many supermarkets. Fresh-cut vegetables prepared in a wok and served over brown rice are appearing in restaurant chains around the country. Some larger cities also have Asian supermarkets, where more specialized foods can be found.

Worldwide Truths

Vegetarian diets are as different as the region or culture they come from, but in general, low-fat, plant-rich diets, with or without small amounts of lean meat, appear to be the healthiest choice for people regardless of culture. However, it is important to remember that diet is not the only factor in a person's overall health. Exercise, smoking, drinking, stress, and income are also factors that affect the health of any individual, whether they eat animal products or not.

Chapter Five

BEGINNING A PLANT-BASED DIET

Decreasing or eliminating meat consumption does not have to be a lifetime commitment; plenty of people give vegetarianism or veganism a try for a while and change their diet if they find it no longer works for them. However, getting the recommended amount of fresh fruits, vegetables, and whole grains is something everyone should make a permanent part of their diet.

Giving up all meat or animal products at once can be a daunting task. Many people begin by giving up beef or pork. From there, they may move on to replacing the chicken in their diet. Eventually, they may stop eating seafood. Finally, some give up eating eggs and dairy products. Exploring vegetarianism and veganism truly is a personal endeavor: There is no one "right" way to do it. If a person chooses to do it, what is most important is doing it in a nutritionally balanced way that has a positive impact on a person's health.

Starting Slow

Cutting out meat is a decision as individual as the person making it. Whatever decision is made and however it is made, it is important to note that it is a personal decision. Respecting other people means respecting their food choices.

In families, where people often share meals, this can sometimes be tricky. Many parents do not have the time or energy to make multiple meals, but not everyone wants to eat vegetarian or vegan. If the entire family is not following the same diet, a cooperative approach may satisfy everyone. Sharing cooking duties is one way to make a family member's transition to a new diet easier on everyone. Mutual consideration also helps. Is the family eating spaghetti and meatballs? Just serve the meatballs on the side and let family members add them to meatless spaghetti sauce if they want to. Does someone want cheese on their casserole? When it is finished, scoop out enough to satisfy the vegans, then sprinkle cheese on the rest. All it takes is a little thought and planning. With a small amount of effort, families can honor each individual's diet.

The journey into a new lifestyle begins with the first step. In the case of vegetarianism or veganism, that means assessing the current situation. Three easy steps will start a person on the path to a healthier lifestyle. First, they can make a list of current vegetarian meals eaten in their

Cooking with a friend can make preparing vegetarian or vegan meals more fun, even if the recipe is complicated.

household. Most families enjoy pasta, pancakes, egg salad sandwiches, and other meatless dishes already, so they can start with what is familiar. When the list is complete, families may be surprised at how many of their eating habits are already compatible with a vegetarian diet. Second, they can list meals that could be vegetarian with just a small alteration. Consider replacing meat sauce with meatless pasta sauce, soy crumbles for ground beef in chili, or vegetable broth instead of chicken broth. Let the family work together so everyone feels involved and honored. Try to make it fun. Know that some substitutions will work and others may not turn out well. Finding the humor in the disasters helps ease tensions and encourages experimentation. Third, they can decide on one or two changes in diet. If a family eats meat frequently, giving it up all at once is going to make everyone feel deprived. Making one or two meals a week vegetarian or vegan is a good way to start slowly.

Experiment with Substitutes

For vegans, some recipes need modifications. Luckily, plenty of choices are out there that make such substitutions simple and tasty. As the popularity of the vegan lifestyle grows, the options available in many grocery stores grow along with it. Many people who give up meat and dairy actually like how these foods taste, so companies have worked hard to create products that are as close to the "real thing" as possible. For example, the Impossible Burger is made from potatoes, wheat, coconut oil, and other plants. However, the addition of a molecule called heme makes it taste just like a beef burger. A similar company called Beyond Meat makes not only burgers but also ground beef and sausage substitutes. However, nutritionists caution that just because these items come from plant sources, it does not mean they should be eaten all the time, especially since the protein in them comes from processed sources rather than whole foods. Registered dietitian nutritionist Robin Foroutan noted, "It's important to keep in mind that things like processed soy and other kinds of processed foods should be eaten in moderation … So, it wouldn't be something that I'd advise people to eat regularly, but certainly for people who are trying to cut down on red meat and that are vegetarians or vegans."[31]

Other foods come close to their animal-derived counterparts as well. Milk comes from a variety of plant sources, including coconuts and almonds. Vegan cheese can be made with a combination of ingredients, including tapioca flour, coconut oil, pea protein, and yeast; some companies proudly advertise that their product tastes just like dairy cheese and even melts the same way—something that was unheard of just a few years ago. Margarine is sometimes marketed as vegan butter.

Additionally, it can be relatively easy to make some common food items vegan by simply replacing one or two ingredients. For example,

The Impossible Burger looks, tastes, and smells like a meat burger, but it is made out of plant proteins.

Meatless Diets and Allergies

For some people, following a completely vegetarian or vegan diet is impossible to do in a healthy way. Many of the most popular, easily accessible replacement foods can trigger allergic reactions in a small segment of the population. For example, if someone is allergic to soy, they cannot eat tofu or tempeh. If they are gluten intolerant, most carbs are off-limits; furthermore, many vegetarian or vegan foods use wheat flour as a thickener, meaning even things such as veggie burgers may trigger a reaction. Avoiding an allergen, just like being vegetarian or vegan, involves carefully reading all labels, asking questions of restaurant staff, and informing friends about specific dietary needs.

According to the North American Vegetarian Society (NAVS), for someone who wants to follow a vegetarian or vegan diet, "it is important to first accurately identify true food sensitivities ... so as to prevent needless elimination of healthful foods. Then, once trigger foods are identified and removed, the main goals are to design a health-supporting diet and to manage ... the food sensitivities."[1] Some people have too many severe allergies to follow a healthy vegan or vegetarian diet, but others can get around their allergy. For example, NAVS noted that people with an allergy to nuts can often substitute seeds such as pumpkin, flax, hemp, sunflower, and sesame to get their required nutrients. Instead of peanut butter, someone might put sunflower seed butter on their sandwich. Anyone who wants to become a vegan or vegetarian should consult a nutritionist, and this is especially true of people with allergies.

1. Dina Aronson, "Food Sensitivities: What's a Vegan Supposed to Do?," North American Vegetarian Society, accessed on July 16, 2019. navs-online.org/articles/food-sensitivities-whats-a-vegan-supposed-to-do/.

many baked goods recipes call for eggs. These can be replaced by a variety of plant-based foods, including applesauce, bananas, and yogurt. Vegan yogurt is available in some grocery stores, but lacto vegetarians can use regular yogurt. One common egg substitute is chia seeds. One tablespoon of chia seeds mixed with three tablespoons of warm water creates a gel that has an egg-like consistency. This ratio should be used for each egg that is being replaced; for example, to replace two eggs, someone would use two tablespoons of chia seeds and six tablespoons of water. Chia seeds have been called a "superfood" because they contain a lot of nutrients, including fiber, healthy fats, calcium, and a variety of vitamins and minerals. This means that using them to replace eggs can actually boost the nutritional content of baked goods, although those baked goods typically still contain sugar. Other items, such as vegan cheese, can also be made at home. For example, cashews blended with water and spices creates a mixture that tastes similar enough to cheese to satisfy many vegans' dairy cravings.

Tofu and tempeh have long been used as meat substitutes, but other options are available as well. For example, when cooked and covered in barbecue sauce, jackfruit can be indistinguishable from pulled pork. Furthermore, portobello burgers, which use a single large portobello mushroom instead of a meat patty, have been on menus for years. Eggplant parmesan has been an alternative to chicken parmesan for decades, but eggplant can also be cut into chunks or sautéed and used in place of chicken in other recipes.

A Closer Look

According to a 2018 article in *Forbes* magazine, prepackaged vegetarian food can contain as much salt as seawater. Fresh food is almost always healthier than processed food, so learning how to cook vegetarian or vegan food is an important part of managing a healthy diet.

Eating Out

Eating at a restaurant or in a school cafeteria can be a challenge for vegetarians and vegans. When they cook at home, they know exactly what goes into their food, but when others serve them, they often have to ask wait staff about the ingredients of menu items. This can feel uncomfortable for both parties, but asking questions is an important way for people to follow the diet that makes them feel best. In many restaurants, a simple change such as leaving the chicken out of a pasta dish can make foods vegetarian-friendly. Some restaurants may even prepare items that are not on the menu if they are asked politely, although customers should not expect this everywhere they go. For instance, In-N-Out Burger, a restaurant chain in the western United States, has a "secret" menu that includes grilled cheese and other vegetarian-friendly choices. However, unless a restaurant caters specifically to vegans, there are likely to be only one or two choices on most menus. For this reason, when choosing a restaurant, many vegans prefer to look at menus online before settling on a place.

School cafeterias also sometimes have vegetarian and vegan options, although generally not many, and a vegetarian or vegan child may find themselves becoming bored with their lunch if they have to buy the same thing every day.

Peanut butter and jelly is a vegetarian lunch, but some schools do not allow students to bring in peanut products because peanut allergies are common.

Eating at the houses of family members or friends can present some challenges too. Planning ahead is the best way to handle this. For example, if someone has recently become vegetarian, they should inform their host before they arrive so the host does not spend a long time making a dinner only to find out that their guest cannot eat any of it.

In most cases, families also like to accommodate their children's friends. A woman named Cheryl Doe summed up the feelings of many when she said, "Just tell me. I really want my kids' friends to feel welcome at our house. I have no problem preparing meatless meals if I know ahead of time."[32]

Keeping Ideals in Mind

Many vegans choose their lifestyle because they care about animals, the environment, and other people. However, cutting out animal products is not an immediate solution to all the problems of the world. For example, quinoa is a grain that is considered a superfood, so it has been in high demand by Westerners—not just vegans and vegetarians, but also people who still eat meat but are looking for other ways to improve their health. However, it has been the source of much controversy in the 2010s. Claims began spreading on the internet that Western demand for the grain caused quinoa prices to rise so much in the grain's native Bolivia and Peru that poor families could no longer afford it, even though it had been a staple of their diet. This distressed many people, some of whom accused vegans and vegetarians of caring more about animals than they did about other people. Many people, regardless of their diet, began to wonder if it was ethical for them to continue to eat quinoa.

In 2016, National Public Radio (NPR) reported that these claims were false. Economists Marc Bellemare and Seth Gitter conducted research into the issue and found that the "claim that rising quinoa prices were hurting those who had traditionally produced and consumed it [is] patently false."[33] However, this does not mean there are no issues with quinoa. Bellemare and other experts noted that the high demand for quinoa could have negative environmental effects. NPR explained,

> Export demand has focused on very few of the 3,000 or so different varieties of quinoa, prompting farmers to abandon many of those varieties. "Those varieties, created by Andean farmers, are the future of quinoa, to adapt to things like climate change," says Stefano Padulosi, a specialist in underused crops ...

Quinoa (shown here) is a small grain that packs a lot of nutrients. However, it has also been the source of much controversy in the 21st century.

A greater ... problem is environmental degradation ... [Economy student] Enrico Avitabile found that more than half the Bolivian farmers he surveyed say their soil is worse than it was before the boom, for two reasons. First, high prices brought into cultivation land that used to be allowed to rest as fallow, resulting in erosion and loss of nutrients. Secondly, farmers who are growing more quinoa, and getting more for it, have reduced their llama herds, so less manure is available as fertilizer and to protect the soil.[34]

Furthermore, the high demand has attracted competitors in other countries, causing the price of Bolivian and Peruvian quinoa to start dropping. This means that farmers who have put their whole livelihood into specialized quinoa crops may eventually suffer. All of this controversy around one single plant food shows that maintaining a vegan or vegetarian diet can involve more work and research than many people think. Furthermore, it is impossible for people to do absolutely zero harm while continuing to live in a way that is comfortable. This does not mean people should commit to being uncomfortable or giving up completely on their ideals, but it is important for everyone to remember that there is only so much any one person can do. For example, some places suffer water shortages, but if people in those areas stop drinking water out of concern for the plants and animals around them, they will eventually die. Sometimes compromises must be made, otherwise people run the risk of allowing concern about their choices to overwhelm them and cause constant emotional distress. Each person must think about the consequences of their choices and decide for themselves which ones they are comfortable living with.

The Cost of a Meatless Diet

As veganism and vegetarianism gain more popularity, substitute foods generally become more affordable. However, for some people, buying fresh fruits and vegetables, meat and dairy substitutes, and other important parts of a vegan or vegetarian diet is not possible all the time. Fresh food tends to be more expensive than processed food, so people who do not have much money are more likely to go for the food they can afford rather than the healthiest options or the options that fit best with a lifestyle choice such as vegetarianism or veganism. Furthermore, people who live in food deserts—areas with high levels of racial segregation and income inequality as well as limited access to healthy food sources—must travel outside their immediate neighborhood to find vegan and vegetarian foods, and without a car or extra money, this can be difficult due to issues such as traveling expenses, traveling with children or a disability, the varying schedules or directness of public transportation, and the weight and logistics of carrying goods back home. According to one student living in a food desert in Washington, D.C., "We mainly live around liquor and snack stores. There aren't that many grocery stores."[35]

While farmers' markets are an excellent place to purchase locally grown produce to support vegetarian and vegan diets, these venues

It is hard to find healthy food at a convenience store or gas station, but for some people, these stores are their only shopping options.

often primarily serve one demographic: white, middle-to-upper class, highly educated consumers. One way to increase the amount of local produce in low-income areas is to bring the farmers' market to the food desert itself.

As food trucks have become more common, some farmers' markets are also going mobile. This allows consumers in many different

low-income neighborhoods access to fresh, local fruits and vegetables. A mobile market must remain affordable for it to benefit people in food deserts who want to eat healthier or try a vegetarian or vegan diet. The U.S. government provides food assistance to low-income families. The two most common programs are the Special Supplemental Nutrition Program for Women, Infants, and Children (WIC) and the Supplemental Nutrition Assistance Program (SNAP). These are sometimes simply called "food stamp" programs because in the past, food assistance came in the form of paper stamps. By 2002, however, these had been replaced by electronic benefits transfer (EBT) cards, which can be swiped at a register like credit cards when buying food. The most successful mobile markets accept payment through WIC or SNAP; some even offer matching programs. All of these efforts combined can make it easier and more affordable for everyone to follow a vegetarian or vegan diet if they choose to.

Another way that people in food deserts can get access to more fruits and vegetables in their diet is through urban gardening programs. Community gardens and school gardens have become popular in cities where fresh produce is not always available, and these gardens provide people with fruits and vegetables that can help them shift toward a more plant-based diet. In addition, community and school gardens serve as a powerful teaching tool. People who tend to these gardens learn about plants and develop a healthier relationship with food and the land, which is often a central part of a vegan or vegetarian lifestyle.

However, it is important to remember that there are a variety of reasons why someone might not follow a vegetarian or vegan diet, with cost and access to fruits and vegetables being common reasons. Just as people should respect an individual's choice to try a vegan or vegetarian diet, an individual's choice not to follow these kinds of diets should also be respected. The reasons people choose not to become vegan or vegetarian are just as varied as the reasons why people choose to follow these lifestyles and go meatless.

Urban gardens are springing up in cities around the world. Vegetables and fruit are grown in areas where people otherwise might not have had access to them.

Following a Beaten Path

Once someone decides to give a plant-based diet a try, there are many resources available to help them take that next step. One of them is speaking with a licensed medical professional. Vegetarians and vegans must remember that their body still needs various vitamins and minerals, as well as protein, fats, and complex carbohydrates, to function properly. Furthermore, some people need medication that comes from animals. For example, gelatin is an animal derivative, so gel capsules are generally avoided by vegans. Vegan.com noted that in some cases, alternatives are available, although they may be more expensive than some people can afford. Even if no substitutions are available or affordable, the website continued,

If you require an animal-derived medicine to treat or manage a serious health issue, it makes sense to take it. You can still accomplish enormous amounts of good based on your dietary choices alone even if you can't be vegan when it comes to your medication. And if you are engaged in even a little vegan advocacy, the contributions you can make by being on earth will certainly far outweigh whatever negative impacts are associated with your medicine's production.[36]

While consuming necessary nutrients as part of a plant-based diet can be done, it will sometimes take some extra effort. New habits can be hard to form. Focusing on specific goals and reasons for exploring a plant-based diet can help someone succeed with their new diet. Eating more fresh fruits, vegetables, and whole grains is a worthy goal regardless of whether someone chooses to give up eating all meat or animal products. In addition, lowering the amount of meat a person consumes is a great way to reduce an individual's impact on the environment while, at the same time, sending a message to CAFOs about how animals should be treated.

Eating fully vegetarian or leading a completely vegan lifestyle can be challenging at times. Sometimes people slip up; they may forget to check a label, not have access to many substitute foods, be very hungry and have no meatless food options around them, or simply be unable to resist a good-looking burger. Getting angry at themselves or at others in these cases is not productive. Instead, they can acknowledge the setback and move forward. No matter why someone starts exploring a plant-based diet or how frequently they engage in it, it can lead to a healthier body, happier animals, and a cleaner planet.

NOTES

Chapter One: Far from a Fad

1. Steven, interview by Susan M. Traugh, November 12, 2009.

2. Mary L. Gavin, ed., "Vegetarianism," KidsHealth, last updated October 2014. kidshealth.org/en/parents/vegetarianism.html.

3. Quoted in Richard Corliss, "Should We All Be Vegetarians?," *TIME*, October 6, 2002. content.time.com/time/magazine/article/0,9171,361598,00.html.

4. Quoted in Associated Press, "Are You a 'Flexitarian?,'" NBC News, March 16, 2004. www.nbcnews.com/id/4541605/ns/health-fitness/t/are-you-flexitarian/.

5. Quoted in Mary Brophy Marcus, "More Young People Go the Vegetarian Route," *USA Today*, November 15, 2007. faunalytics.org/wp-content/uploads/2015/05/Citation542.pdf.

6. Elisabeth, interview by Susan M. Traugh, November 12, 2009.

Chapter 2: Why Give Up Meat?

7. Quoted in Daniel J. DeNoon, "Metabolic Syndrome Common in Obese Children," WebMD, June 25, 2008. www.webmd.com/children/news/20080625/obese-kids-metabolic-syndrome-common#1.

8. John Messmer, "The Lowdown on Sugar: Is Sugar as Unhealthy as Everyone Claims?," Diet Channel, October 25, 2006. www.thedietchannel.com/the-Low-down-on-sugar.htm.

9. Rosane Oliveira, "Diet and Diabetes: Why Saturated Fats Are the Real Enemy," UC Davis Integrative Medicine, September 14, 2016. ucdintegrativemedicine.com/2016/09/diet-diabetes-saturated-fats-real-enemy/.

10. Oliveira, "Diet and Diabetes."

11. Oliveira, "Diet and Diabetes."

12. William Harris, "Cancer and the Vegetarian Diet," Vegsource, December 21, 1999. vegsource.com/harris/cancer_vegdiet.htm.

13. "Vegetarian and Vegan Diets," American Institute for Cancer Research, accessed on June 9, 2019. www.aicr.org/patients-survivors/healthy-or-harmful/vegetarian-and-vegan.html.

14. Samantha Cassidy, "What a Nutritionist Wants You to Know About Pesticides and Produce," NBC News, last updated April 15, 2018. www.nbcnews.com/better/health/produce-side-pesticides-what-nutritionist-wants-you-know-about-ewg-ncna864156.

15. Elisabeth, interview by Susan M. Traugh, November 12, 2009.

16. Lierre Keith, *The Vegetarian Myth: Food, Justice, and Sustainability*. Crescent City, CA: Flashpoint, 2009, p. 1.

17. Keith, *The Vegetarian Myth*, p. 3.

18. Emma Henderson, "Why Veganism Isn't as Environmentally Friendly as You Might Think," *Independent*, January 27, 2018. www.independent.co.uk/life-style/food-and-drink/veganism-environment-veganuary-friendly-food-diet-damage-hodmedods-protein-crops-jack-monroe-a8177541.html.

19. Henderson, "Why Veganism Isn't as Environmentally Friendly as You Might Think."

Chapter 3: Nutrition Without Meat

20. Patty Knutson, "Let's Uncover the Truth Behind the Vegan Food Pyramid," Vegan Coach, accessed on July 11, 2019. www.vegancoach.com/vegan-food-pyramid.html.

21. Alena, "The Vegan Food Pyramid: Full Guide to Meeting Your Nutrients," Nutriciously, February 19, 2018. nutriciously.com/vegan-food-pyramid/.

22. Quoted in Corliss, "Should We All Be Vegetarians?"

23. Matt, interview by Susan M. Traugh, November 12, 2009.

24. Stephen Walsh, "What Every Vegan Should Know About Vitamin B12," Vegan Society, October 2001. www.vegansociety.com/resources/nutrition-and-health/nutrients/vitamin-b12/what-every-vegan-should-know-about-vitamin-b12.

25. Walsh, "What Every Vegan Should Know."

Chapter 4: A Cross-Cultural Phenomenon

26. Soutik Biswas, "The Myth of the Indian Vegetarian Nation," BBC, April 4, 2018. www.bbc.com/news/world-asia-india-43581122.

27. Biswas, "The Myth of the Indian Vegetarian Nation."

28. Quoted in Biswas, "The Myth of the Indian Vegetarian Nation."

29. Biswas, "The Myth of the Indian Vegetarian Nation."

30. Quoted in Mitsuru Kakimoto, "Vegetarianism and Vegetarians in Japan," IVU News, 1998. www.ivu.org/news/3-98/japan1.html.

Chapter 5: Beginning a Plant-Based Diet

31. Quoted in Erica Sweeney, "Are Beyond Meat and Impossible Burgers Better for You? Nutritionists Weigh In," *HuffPost*, July 10, 2019. www.huffpost.com/entry/beyond-meat-impossible-burger-healthy_l_5d164ad1e4b07f6ca57cc3ed.

32. Cheryl Doe, interview by Susan M. Traugh, November 11, 2009.

33. Quoted in Jeremy Cherfas, "Your Quinoa Habit Really Did Help Peru's Poor. But There's Trouble Ahead," NPR, March 31, 2016. www.npr.org/sections/thesalt/2016/03/31/472453674/your-quinoa-habit-really-did-help-perus-poor-but-theres-trouble-ahead.

34. Cherfas, "Your Quinoa Habit."

35. Quoted in Paige Pfleger, "Healthy Eaters, Strong Minds: What School Gardens Teach Kids," NPR, August 10, 2015. www.npr.org/sections/thesalt/2015/08/10/426741473/healthy-eaters-strong-minds-what-school-gardens-teach-kids.

36. "Vegan FAQ: Answers to Frequently Asked Questions," Vegan.com, accessed on July 16, 2019. www.vegan.com/faq.

ORGANIZATIONS TO CONTACT

American Public Health Association (APHA)
800 I Street NW
Washington, DC 20001
www.apha.org
twitter.com/PublicHealth

APHA is an organization that works to protect the health of Americans through programs that provide education and preventive health services to communities.

Animal Welfare Institute (AWI)
900 Pennsylvania Avenue SE
Washington, DC 20003
awionline.org
twitter.com/AWIOnline
www.youtube.com/user/animalwelfarevideos

AWI works to reduce the suffering of animals used in agriculture and research—for instance, by replacing factory farms with humane, family-run farms. It also campaigns against brutal methods of fur trapping and for protection of wildlife.

North American Vegetarian Society
P.O. Box 72
Dolgeville, NY 13329
navs-online.org
www.facebook.com/WorldVegetarianDay

This nonprofit organization promotes veganism as a healthy, cruelty-free, sustainable lifestyle.

The Vegan Society
Donald Watson House
34 35 Ludgate Hill
Birmingham, England
B3 1EH
www.vegansociety.com
www.instagram.com/theoriginalvegansociety
twitter.com/TheVeganSociety
www.youtube.com/user/TheVeganSociety
> This British nonprofit organization offers tips and health information
> for people who want to eat vegan.

The Vegetarian Resource Group (VRG)
PO Box 1463
Baltimore, MD 21203
vrg.org
vrg@vrg.org
> The VRG has recipes and articles especially for teens and information
> for vegans.

Books

Boothroyd, Jennifer. *Why Doesn't Everyone Eat Meat?: Vegetarianism and Special Diets*. Minneapolis, MN: Lerner Publications Company, 2016.
This book explores alternative diets, including vegetarianism and veganism.

Elton, Sarah, and Julie McLaughlin. *Meatless?: A Fresh Look at What You Eat*. Berkeley, CA: Owlkids Books, Inc., 2017.
This book looks at all the various reasons why people choose to cut meat out of their diet and the culture of being vegetarian or vegan.

Gleeson, Erin. *The Forest Feast for Kids: Colorful Vegetarian Recipes That Are Simple to Make*. New York, NY: Abrams Books for Young Readers, 2016.
This cookbook from food blogger Erin Gleeson offers vegetarian recipes anyone can make.

Perdew, Laura. *Animal Rights Movement*. North Mankato, MN: Abdo Publishing Company, 2014.
The author examines various aspects of the animal rights movement.

Turnbull, Sam. *Fuss-Free Vegan: 101 Everyday Comfort Food Favorites, Veganized*. Westminster, MD: Appetite by Random House, 2017.
This cookbook shows people how to make vegan versions of their favorite foods.

Websites
Humane Farming Association (HFA)
www.hfa.org
> This organization is dedicated to reducing cruelty to farm animals and ending the practice of factory farming.

Happy Cow
www.happycow.net
> This website helps vegans and vegetarians find restaurants near them, both at home and while they are traveling. It also includes articles on vegan topics, such as vegan airline meals and tips for getting started in the lifestyle, as well as forums to help like-minded people connect. Always ask a parent or guardian before posting in an online forum.

KidsHealth: Food and Fitness
kidshealth.org/en/teens/food-fitness
> The articles on this section of the KidsHealth website cover the basics of a healthy lifestyle, including nutrition and exercise information. In the section "Problems with Food and Exercise," visitors can learn about eating disorders, body image, helping friends with eating disorders, and more.

Meatless Monday
www.meatlessmonday.com
> Even if someone cannot or does not want to go completely meatless, reducing meat consumption can have a positive impact on both health and the environment. This website, which promotes eating vegetarian or vegan at least one day each week, offers many recipes and resources.

Vegan.com
> This website offers information about all aspects of veganism.

INDEX

PICTURE CREDITS

Jason Brainard was the head day cook at vegetarian restaurant Preservation Hall when the Buffalo, New York, alternative weekly paper *Artvoice* voted it the "Best Place to Have Brunch" in 1999. The evening cooks were not impressed.